CAST OFF

a collection of Shakespeare themed stories.

MARGARET EGROT

ALL RIGHTS RESERVED

No part of this book may be reproduced or transmitted in
any form or by any means, electronic or mechanical,
including photocopying, recording, or by any information
storage and retrieval system, without permission in writing
from the author, except in the case of brief quotations
embodied in reviews.

Publisher's Note:

This is a work of fiction. All names, characters, places, and
events are the work of the author's imagination.

Any resemblance to real persons, places, or events is
coincidental.

Solstice Publishing - www.solsticepublishing.com

Copyright 2017 – Margaret Egrot

Cast Off

A Collection of
Shakespeare Themed Stories

Margaret Egrot

Dedication

To my father, Ted Cowen, who loved his Shakespeare.

"Comparisons are odorous"
(Dogberry, Act 111, Scene 5, Much Ado About Nothing)

CW00952951

Table of Cont

Foreword

Have you ever thought what a Shakespeare character might be thinking or doing before she comes on stage? Does she like the role that's been created for her? Would she prefer a different plot? Or love interest? How does she really feel about all that cross dressing?

In this collection of short stories, the central character is always one of the female characters from a play by William Shakespeare. There is no need to be familiar with the play to enjoy the story but, for anyone who is, a number of quotations and references should elicit the occasional smile of recognition. Be warned though, sometimes a quotation will be from a completely different play.

Each story stands alone, and each character featured in them is important in her particular play, but she is not necessarily a leading figure. Some of them appear only peripherally—if at all. In *Ban! Ban! Cacaliban!* for example, Sycorax, the witch, never actually appears on stage in *The Tempest*. But she is talked about by other characters and she is important because she is the mother of the oafish Caliban, and a previous 'ruler' of the island before the benign Prospero. She and Caliban are, in fact, the antitheses of Shakespeare's protagonist and his lovely daughter, Miranda.

Cassandra, in *Our Mad Sister*, hardly appears on stage, and is dismissed by all as crazy. But she is the only one who seems to know what's going to happen, so it would have been worth the others paying more attention to her. (Though of course, if that had happened, it would have been a completely different tale that Shakespeare would have drawn on for *Troilus and Cressida*). Hermione, in *The*

Ghost Queen, spends most of *The Winter's Tale* supposedly dead, but it was her sudden 'death' that was the catalyst for her husband's remorse. The young woman, in *Journey to the Fair Mountain* seems to have been smitten with the wrong brother when she arrives through the winter snow at her intended husband's castle in Elsinore (*Hamlet*).

In some of the stories, the character chosen has a leading role in the play, but Kate (*The Taming of the Shrew*), spends most of *Is Not This Well?* arguing with the Bard for a more feminist story-line. Lady Macbeth, in *Look to the Lady*, is depicted writing a love letter to her husband whilst he is away fighting, and Desdemona, after one meeting with Othello, spends the night in *Chains of Magic* imagining how she can entrap him, through food (or magic) into falling in love with her. In *Conjuring the Moon,* the naïve, and somewhat priggish, Cordelia's relationship with her older sisters is imagined before Lear summons them to share out the country between them and, in *A Virtuous Maid* (*Measure for Measure*), Isabella's enthusiasm for being a bride of Christ rather than a flesh and blood male's, falters surprisingly quickly.

In a few stories, the character is seen through the eyes of another. Olivia's feelings and behaviour, in *The Tangled Knot* (*Twelfth Night*), are explained, with generous dollops of psychobabble, by the clown, and Hermia's emotions in *A Midsummer Day's Dream* are re-lived by the actress playing her in a student production. A young carer, in *Time out of Mind*, looks after an old lady with dementia who may or may not have played a significant role in the lives of the doomed lovers, Romeo and Juliet, and in *The Quality of Mirth* (*The Merchant of Venice*), Portia's maid, Nerissa, fills her diary, when she can spare a moment, with thrilled accounts of her mistress's exploits.

Thirteen stories in all—a baker's dozen, in case one fails to please. The more serious-minded Shakespeare scholars might disapprove of what I've written, but they probably wouldn't have picked up this collection of stories in the first place. However, if you've read this far, I do hope that you will go on to read the stories - and that you will enjoy them.

Is Not This Well?

I felt I had to put a stop to it. Making people laugh is all very well; but not at my expense it isn't. Besides, his proposed plot was bound to spoil his reputation one day, when people became more sensitive about such matters. I felt he should be more careful, even though, seeing as this was early days in his career, he didn't have much of a reputation to spoil. However, it was my character he was slagging off, and I had a right to look out for my own reputation, nevermind his.

His study door was open and I marched straight in without knocking, which I knew he hated, and put both hands on the back of his chair.

"Why do you want to write a play that will make you look like a mis... a mis..." I started.

"Misogynist?" he filled in, slapping down his quill impatiently.

He was always like that. Good with words, even ones that were not yet in common use. And if he couldn't find the right word—well, he just made one up!

I nodded. Misogynist sounded like just the word I was looking for. Having given me the word, he shrugged dismissively and, picking up his quill again, turned back to his writing. I poked him sharply. So what if he hated being interrupted when he was working, he still hadn't answered my question.

"Why do you want to look like a misogynist, and why do you have to portray me as such a cow in the process? You know me well enough by now; I don't mind playing a feisty character if that's what you want - give as good as I get and all that jazz. But you're making me out to be a monster."

He shook his head crossly, and a small spray of dead skin floated from his scalp. He really ought to do something about that bald patch, I thought, as I brushed the dandruff from the front of my dress with theatrical sweeps. Also I noted, but only to myself, by letting his hair grow all long and wispy around the sides he was only drawing attention to it.

"You've got to be larger than life and frighten all the men away, or the rest of the play won't work," he said, without stopping writing.

"I'm okay with that," I conceded grudgingly, but I wasn't letting him off the hook yet. "But why do I have to be such a shrew as well?"

He paused again and turned towards me. This time his face lit up. He really is quite good looking when he smiles, even with a flaky pate.

"Thanks Kate," he said, and I'd have sworn he was about to reach round and pat my bum till he remembered what happened last time. "You've given me a great idea for the title."

He turned his back again, shuffled through his papers till he came to the first page, and re-inked his quill. He scratched out the title at the top and wrote instead in big bold letters. *The Taming of the Shrew.* I don't think I've ever actually thumped him before, but it was bound to happen sooner or later.

"Ouch!" A squirt of ink shot across his manuscript as my fist landed between his shoulder blades. He mopped at it hastily with an old rag.

"Now look what you've done! You'll never get a husband behaving like this, my girl. This scene is useless now, you'd scare the pants off the lot of them. I'll have to create a much stronger character with a temper to match yours, if I'm going to marry you off before the end of the play."

"Oh, go boil your ears!" I was rather proud of that

exclamation. If he wasn't so cross with me for thumping him, maybe he would remember the phrase and use it in another play one day. Maybe even give me credit for it, though that was unlikely. Not that I was bothered just then. He could have written me out of this play, then and there, for all I cared. I tipped his ink pot over to make my feelings even clearer, and stomped off.

"Damn you," his voice followed me down the stairs. "I'm going to have to get a lock put on that damn door, or I'll never get this damn play finished."

For a wordsmith, his own use of expletives was quite limited really.

***

Curiosity got the better of me by the end of the day and I couldn't go to bed without finding out what he'd been up to since I left him. *Was I still the central character? Or had he had a change of tack and gone for some soppy, submissive heroine?* Again I entered his study without knocking—he obviously hadn't got round to putting a lock on yet.

He'd been busy all right. The floor was strewn with crumpled paper, and it looked as if he had worn out two quills with all his scribbling. On his desk was a neat pile of completed pages, held down by an old skull he always used as a paper weight.

But the bard, himself, was not working. He was stretched out in his easy chair in the corner of his study. His feet were on the hearth almost in the fire, his mouth was slack, and he was snoring sonorously. Worn out writing bitchy stuff for me to perform, I thought grimly. *Why did I have to be a termagant?* I could still be forceful, but more on the lines of female characters he was to conjure up in the future: pretty, plucky, confident ladies, who couldn't wait for the first act to be over before finding an excuse to dress up in rather fetching boys' clothes, and having a high old time romping round the stage for the rest of the play?

What had he got in store for me exactly? How much had he changed since our encounter this morning? I just had to know. I touched him gently and called his name softly. No response. He seemed in a deep, deep, sleep. *No harm in having a quick peep, surely?* I tiptoed across the wooden floor, willing the old boards not to creek and reached his desk successfully without making a sound. I noted with some pride how far the ink had splashed out across his desk after I'd toppled the ink pot in the morning. It would have taken him a while to clear that up before he could start working again. Give him pause for thought.

The skull seemed to leer at me, daring me to move it and shift through his papers.

"Sod you," I mouthed, and reached out my hand.

"Don't even think about it!"

How could someone wake from such a deep sleep without making a sound? I spun round.

"As if I would!"

He looked fully alert, and amused rather than angry with me—which was perhaps more annoying.

"You know I wouldn't mess up your papers, Will. But you've got to tell me what you've got planned. Are you going to have me play the shrew throughout, or do I get a bit of depth?" He was about to reply, but I held my hand up to stop him.

"Just as important, what kind of a man have you got in store for me? If you just want a Punch and Judy knock about, you can find yourself another puppet."

"Kate, Kate! Don't forget you've already messed my papers up today, so what worth can I put on your word? Took me ages to clean it all up, but it gave me time to think. You're right. I need a more rounded, fleshed out character, not just an angry cypher. And I need a suitor to match. I'm still setting the play in Italy, my Katherina, but that's as near as we get to puppet comedy. Satisfied now?"

I sort of nodded, and he patted the chair next to his. "So, if you've nothing better to do, Sweet Lady, come sit by me and I'll tell you what I'm planning."

'Sweet Lady?' He writes irony, better than he speaks it! But his offer sounded genuine, and as I didn't really have anything better to do before bedtime. I bit my tongue and sat down.

***

"There'll be a suitor for you, of course," he said, once I was sitting next to him. "A strong character, a match for your temper. Difficult to decide what to call him though. Most of these Italian names are a bit soppy—like Baptista! That's the name I've chosen for your dad, by the way, but he's a bit on the wimpy side, so it suits him. Anyway, I've come up with the name Petruchio for your swain. How does that appeal to you?"

I shrugged non-committedly, not sure where this conversation was going, but he took it as agreement.

"This Petruchio's dad has died," he went on. "So he's come into his inheritance and he's decided it's time to settle down and find a wife. He's not too fussy, just so long as she comes from the same class, and brings in a bit of money."

"Ta very much! Not a love match then?" I snorted.

"No. Not at the start anyway. He'll need to knock you into shape first."

"Now hold it right there. Do you mean he's going to literally knock me about? That's no way to treat a woman. Ever. And if you think that's the sort of thing you need to make the audience laugh, I'm walking out right now."

Will, looked at me for a while whilst I glared at him.

"I can't see what your problem is. You thumped me earlier today, remember? And I haven't heard you raise any objection to bashing your own family and other suitors around in the first act. Lighten up, Kate. It's only a play, after all."

I got up quickly, sniffed loudly, and made for the door. He put out a restraining hand.

"Oh, all right, I'll have a look at that scene again." He got up, shuffled over to his desk, and returned with the manuscript, quill and inkpot. He put the inkpot carefully on the other side of his chair, out of my reach, and sifted through his papers for a while.

"How about, if he just threatens to cuff you once, but never does it? Please, Kate, it's still the sixteenth century, and you have just struck him. I can't have him supporting you in your career, hanging out the washing, and changing nappies. He's got to convince as a man of his time. And, admit it, a woman with your character is not going to fall for a sensitive dreamer, who boasts about how in touch with his feminine side he is, are you?"

That made me laugh. Will can be surprisingly insightful at times.

"Point taken. But just the once, and just the threat. I'll live with that." He beamed at me, and scribbled onto his script.

"So," I said, when he'd finished writing. "This Petruchio fellow's determined to have me, sight unseen. What on earth is going to induce me to marry him on the basis of one meeting?"

"Because, underneath all your bravado, you're just an ordinary girl, and you're desperate. You're getting on a bit, you can't stand living with your drippy old dad, and you're jealous of your little sister who's getting all the attention because everybody thinks she's adorable, whereas you know better. You can't bear the thought of being left on the shelf, but you know all the men hanging around the house for your sister are not good enough for you. Then along comes a chap who's as bold as brass and isn't put off by your sharp tongue—well he has to be worth considering."

"You get all that across in our first scene?" I exclaim, incredulously.

"Try to," he smirked, modestly. "Are you with me so far?"

"Hmm." I was still a bit doubtful about his portrayal of woman as a commodity that could be bought so easily. Passed from father to husband so long as the price is right. But playing opposite this Petruchio character could be fun.

"What next?"

Will and I talked into the night. He was determined that the way Petruchio was to win me round was a series of humiliating scenes, masquerading as care. I was determined that a modern woman, at the turn of the century, was not just a punch bag, or the butt of male humour

"Look at it the other way round, Kate. Here is a man who doesn't want a simpering wife. He wants someone his intellectual, social, and temperamental equal. He has to impress you with his own strong character. Just look what you did to the posturing Hortensio. He doesn't want you doing that do him, and you wouldn't respect him if he was the kind of man you could do that to. Now would you?"

"Can't say," I had to admit. "You haven't told me what I'm supposed to have done to this Hortensio character."

"Oh, he comes a wooing your sister in the play and you smash a lute over his head."

I burst out laughing at this. He's right, I'm certainly not going to fall for a soppy musician. Will laughs too.

"See! It's my aim to make you a great comic creation—but as Petruchio's equal, not at the expense of your dignity. Once you get the measure of him, you go along with his cranky behaviour, and a strangely supportive alliance against the others develops between you. By the end of the play, this will seem truer and more lasting than their sighing and protestations of undying love, I promise you."

"Not exactly a manifesto of female equality though?"

"Come off it. I'm writing a comedy, not a social tract."

It was getting late, and I suddenly felt really tired. I yawned and stood up.

"Jeez, Will, I'm knackered. I'm going to have to turn in or I'll fall asleep in this chair."

"Me too. And I've got to get up early to finish this play, now we're agreed on how it develops. After all, we're scheduled to start rehearsals tomorrow afternoon, and first performance on Monday."

I shrugged. "I'm not sure I've agreed to anything. But I know you've got to come up with something pretty sharpish to put on stage, or we'll all be out of work. I suppose I'll just have to trust you to do okay by me."

"I will," he put his hand out to me. "Friends?"

I took his hand. "Friends," I agreed, and meant it.

I left him then. I'd done my best to inject a modern, feminist, slant into his thinking, but it wasn't really my prerogative to insist he write a play that would stand the test of time. Anyway, a lot can be done by the actors and the way they interpret their parts.

***

And, gosh, the audience didn't half laugh on opening night, so he succeeded in writing a great comedy all right. I'm still not sure about the title though. And don't get me started on that closing speech.

"I ran out of time for more changes," he told me, quite unabashed, when I challenged him. I'm sure there's a word for men like that.

A Midsummer Day's Dream

"You're welcome."

Mia Cross smiled her thanks to the barman then, with purse tucked under her arm and a glass of wine in each hand, she hobbled back out into the glare of the midday sun. Her feet were hot and sweaty, and she could feel the skin on both little toes chafing, adding to the pain she was already experiencing from an old blister on her right heel that had burst back into angry life earlier in the morning. It was stupid to wear heels on such a hot day but, with Helen being so tall, Mia liked to give herself a bit of a lift when she was out with her. At least, in these shoes, she came up to Helen's ear rather than her chin.

The strapless sundress may have been a mistake too, her inner monologue continued, the fierce sun prickling her already pink skin as she walked across the beer garden. I'm going to look a complete mess tonight: limping about the stage with a face and shoulders the colour of a ripe pomegranate.

Helen, however, seemed oblivious to her friend's suffering; as she was to any effects the midday heat was having on her own skin. Despite Mia's approach, Helen remained slumped in her chair staring glumly at the grain in the sturdy, wooden picnic table, an empty glass in front of her.

Mia put the wine down carefully and slid the larger glass across the table to her friend.

"Here, get this down you. But don't drink it as fast as the last one. I don't know what the matter is, but getting sloshed right now isn't going to make things any better."

Helen grunted. Mia wasn't sure if it was a grunt of agreement or dissent, as Helen just raised the new glass to her lips without lifting her eyes. But Mia was relieved to notice she only took a small sip this time. Mia herself was already feeling a bit tipsy from the last glass. She never could handle much alcohol, especially so early in the day after a breakfast that had been skimpy to say the least. She would definitely make this one last, and stick to soft drinks when the boys arrived. She sat down opposite her friend and, with a faint sigh of relief, slipped out of her shoes gently rubbing each sore toe in turn against the sole of the opposite foot. The grass beneath the table was cool and soothing under her feet.

The girls sat in silence for several minutes; Helen drinking steadily, Mia hardly touching hers. She looked at her friend doubtfully, willing her to look up and say something—anything. I don't care how miserable she is, she decided as the silence continued, alcohol isn't improving matters and I'm not buying her another drink. Anyway, I know it's not my fault, not really.

Helen and Mia had been friends at school, virtually inseparable since the age of five. Indeed in their last year their English teacher, who perhaps should have known better in these sensitive times, had described the pair of them as a double cherry—"two lovely berries, moulded on one stem," he had declaimed in front of the whole class. Hearing about this, the headmistress had called him to her study, and was only partially reassured when he explained that it was a quote from Shakespeare—*A Midsummer Night's Dream* no less—and that he'd said it during the course of a drama lesson. Mia and Helen, he had added hastily as the Head continued to frown, were his star pupils, keen as mustard, and definitely good enough to go on to drama school after their A levels, as they said they wanted to.

He had been right about that, anyway. The pair of them had applied successfully to the Royal College of Performing Arts and here they were, approaching the end of their first year, still seemingly inseparable. But Helen had become monumentally miserable in the last few weeks, just as Mia felt a whole new exciting world was opening up in front of her; mostly in the shape of Lenny.

Ah, Lenny! He was generally agreed to be the fittest guy in this year's drama intake. She had fancied him from day one, but been too shy to do anything except admire him from a distance. And things could easily have stayed like that, with only the occasional friendly nod from him if they passed each other on the college steps, to fuel her fantasies. However, the drama tutor responsible for the end of year performance, inadvertently casting herself in the role of Cupid, had nominated them to play one of the pairs of lovers in *A Midsummer Night's Dream*. And solid fact was steadily, incredibly, wonderfully, taking its cue from the dramatic fiction. Talk about a dream come true!

Mia could still hardly believe it, and smiled to herself as she took a tiny sip from her glass. It had at first been a disappointment—to have to repeat the play that she and Helen had done in their last year at school, when she had played Titania and Helen had been Oberon (it was an all-girls school not an avant-garde performance so, somewhat predictably, all the tall girls had been obliged to take male roles). But once she and Lenny had become an item she had decided that it was a play she would want to act in to celebrate their meeting every single mid-summer until she died.

When he first arrived at the college, Lenny, with his ready smile and seemingly boundless energy, had swiftly become the centre of a large, mostly male and sporty seeming, social circle. This included Dennis who, it transpired, came from the same city although they hadn't known each other properly before meeting again at the college, as they had gone to different schools at opposite ends of the city. Dennis, apparently, lived at the posh end. But they had quickly worked out that they had played against each other in at least two inter-school rugby games, though their recollections differed as to which school actually won on each occasion.

In Mia's opinion, Lenny was the most beautiful human being ever put on this earth. She smiled again as she thought about him, and how quickly things had moved since that first memorable rehearsal. How she loved to run her fingers over his cheeks and round the contours of the muscles in his arms. And when he touched her... she closed her eyes briefly as a frisson of remembered passion swept over her. She could barely wait for the holidays when, once lectures and this production were out of the way, they would have more time to be on their own without other students around. He had already promised to visit her at home—though she wasn't too sure what her father, whose political heroes were somewhat to the right of Genghis Khan, would make of a tall, black hunk knocking on his front door and announcing he was his daughter's boyfriend. After all Mr. and Mrs. Cross had plenty of friends who had, Mr. Cross would often say, a propos of nothing in particular, several suitable sons with good social backgrounds and potential earning capacities similar to his own, for his daughter to choose from.

Mr. Cross didn't go along with all these different foreign cultures springing up everywhere, he would tell anyone not yet completely comatose at the table, after one of his wife's wine fueled and protracted Sunday lunches. But there was a lot to say for those arranged marriages some immigrants were into. At least you knew what you were getting for a son-in-law. Mia was fond of her father, but really, he was impossible! Not, of course, that she and Lenny were planning to get married. Much too early days for that kind of thinking.

But thinking of Lenny now led inevitably to thinking of Dennis. And then to why Helen was so miserable. She simply had to get Helen to talk. It might clear the air, or at least get her out of the pit of despair and self-pity that she seemed to have dug for herself. If not, she could ruin everything for the four of them.

When Helen lifted her glass again, Mia put out a restraining arm.

"Being sloshed isn't going to help," she repeated.

"Get stuffed." Helen jerked away from Mia and carried on drinking. But at least she had spoken, so Mia decided to plough on.

"Want to talk about it?"

Helen shook her head, and turned away to avoid her friend's concerned stare. The pair sat in silence for several more minutes, until Mia couldn't bear it any longer.

"It's Dennis isn't it?"

"You tell me." Helen turned on her friend with such viciousness, that Mia flinched.

"Look, I've said I'm sorry. It didn't mean anything. We just got a bit drunk and silly after we got shitty marks for that last essay. But there's nothing in it I promise you. Besides, I'm with Lenny now, and he's not bothered, so why should you be? As for Dennis, it's you he's always fancied. Surely, you know that?"

"Well, you tell me. Tell me why he hasn't called me once since that night, ignores all my texts, hardly notices me when we meet, and tags along with Lenny whenever he can, just to see you."

"Honestly Helen, you don't need to worry about me and him. It's just Lenny and me now. We've made plans for the summer and all—and Dennis the Menace doesn't feature in any of them."

"Someone needs to tell him then, because he obviously sees things very differently. I bet he will be along now when Lenny arrives."

"Well of course he will, stupid. Lenny wants us to go over that scene in the woods together to get the actions spot on. He's got some new idea—says it's no use just saying the words. He wants us to 'make a statement' or something and we've got to make sure we're standing in the right places on stage and move on cue, or it won't work. It's supposed to be a comedy, remember. And Lenny thinks we can add dramatic impact or something. I'm sorry I'm a bit vague, but you know Lenny when he has an idea—words flow and you get carried away with his enthusiasm without really knowing what he's on about. All I know is he thinks it'll work, and add to the dramatic punch of the scene. But it'll take off like a lead balloon if we don't get it right—and that won't go down well with the judges, or help our careers. So you've just got to buck your ideas up or we're all fucked."

"I don't feel in the least bit like laughing, making other people laugh, or making an impact on anyone or anything except Dennis."

"Of course you don't. Not now, anyway. So you'll have to try acting, my dear. The. Show. Must. Go. On!"

"Piss off."

"Helen, I'm really sorry. Shall I try speaking to him again, if you think it'll help? Or get Lenny to?"

"Fat lot of good that will be. He seems to prefer you snapping at him to me doting on him. I'd do anything to get him to love me again, but he just ignores me."

"Well try ignoring him back. And stop crying. He certainly isn't going to fancy you with red eyes and your skin all blotchy. Here use this tissue and give yourself a tidy up. They'll be here any minute."

Helen took the proffered hanky and blew her nose noisily.

"Maybe if I could look and speak more like you, he'd fancy me again."

"Try scowling at him—seems to work for me! Oh Helen, I'm sorry, I didn't mean to be flippant. It's just—I'm in love with a guy who loves me back, and I can't help sounding happy. I'm sure things will work out for you, too. With Lenny and me out of the way, as soon as term ends, you'll have the field to yourself."

Mia was increasingly aware that her words were not providing Helen with a shred of comfort, and quite possibly making things worse, but she couldn't stop herself. She was relieved therefore to look up and see the two young men coming across the beer garden towards them, Dennis first, Lenny a little behind as, from what she could make out, he had stopped at the gate to shake a small pebble out of his sandal.

Dennis greeted Mia enthusiastically and nodded briefly to Helen.

"Drinks anyone?" he asked, looking only at Mia.

"Not for me, thanks. I'm making this one last. But Helen's glass is nearly empty."

"And you can get a pint in for me too—the usual," Lenny said, as he arrived. He kissed Mia and sat next to her, an arm slung proprietorially round her shoulders. Dennis looked at them both, with a slight tightening of his lips, then turned to go to the bar.

"Wait! Another dry white wine for me—I'll come with you." Helen scrambled to her feet and made to follow him.

"Don't bother, I can manage." He didn't slow his pace, and Helen shrank back down into her seat. Mia and Lenny exchanged glances. Things didn't augur well for their rehearsal, let alone the show tonight. As tradition would have it, the first year students' play was the precursor to the dean's midsummer eve reception, and all the famous, or semi famous, alumni who had made names for themselves in the theatre were invited, as well as assorted critics and journalists and, of course, the judges of the individual performances, stage direction, scenery and props. Each student was offered two tickets so they could invite their parents or other relatives. Mia was glad her parents couldn't make it. In fact, none of their parents could come; only Lenny's aunt who had something to do with the theatre in her own right, intended to be there.

Lenny took out a hanky and mopped his brow.

"Jeez, it's a scorcher today," he said. "I think it's going to be too hot to think properly if we stay sitting here. Let's take ourselves over to those trees at the far end of the garden. At least we'll get a bit of shade there."

Mia nodded enthusiastically.

"The scene's set in the woods, too. We can use the trees as props—make the rehearsal more realistic." She scooped up her shoes from under the table as Lenny pulled her to her feet.

"It's only the moves I want to change—we should all be word perfect by now."

"Oh we are, we are, aren't we Helen? Just anxious to know what your killer idea is. Ouch, stop tickling me."

Lenny and Mia ran, laughing, towards the little copse. Helen dawdled at the table, justifying to herself that it would be where Dennis would return when he came back from the bar, and she could lead him to where the others had gone. Maybe if she also told him about Mia's and Lenny's plans for the summer he would see that there was nothing doing for him with Mia, and maybe....

But Dennis had already spotted Lenny and Mia heading down towards the trees and walked briskly after them with the tray of drinks, bypassing the table completely. There was nothing for her to stay for now, so Helen trailed sadly in his wake, like a whipped puppy.

***

"Act Three, scene two," said Lenny who, by general consent, had taken the lead in orchestrating all their extra rehearsals. "Puck and Oberon are hiding in the wings, so we don't need to bother about them except that they give the clue as to how I think we must play this scene. I thought about it a few nights ago and I really think it will bring something to the set up, which all the audience are likely to have seen loads of times already. It's when Puck says—'Shall we their *pageant* see? Lord what *fools* these mortals be!'—That's where my idea comes from. Everybody's used to seeing this scene played with an emphasis on *foolish,* and all the actors running round being silly. But I think, we should emphasise the *pageantry,* without losing the comic aspects of course. If we can pull that off—do something completely different—the judges can only be impressed."

"But how do we do that?" Dennis sounded doubtful.

"Yes, tell us how we are going to do that?" Mia was also doubtful, but didn't want to dampen Lenny's enthusiasm.

"I want you guys to help me with this," Lenny said, flashing his most engaging smile round the three of them. "But for starters we make use of Helen's height. You're so tall and elegant, Helen, you're just made for a masque."

Helen started. She hadn't really been following the discussion and wondered if Lenny was making fun of her. She was even more disconcerted when Dennis suddenly looked at her properly for the first time in weeks, and nodded in agreement.

"Ah, I see where you're coming from. We're going to stage it as a pageant round her. Helen, you'd be absolutely grand, standing centre stage whilst we circle and develop the word play around you. That's your idea, isn't it?"

Lenny nodded. "Got it in one."

Helen smiled doubtfully as if, having yearned for weeks for Dennis to pay her some attention, she was finding his interest in her now rather unsettling. Or maybe it was just the wine making her feel a little dizzy.

Lenny too was staring at her speculatively.

"That's the idea," he agreed, turning back to Dennis. "Especially when you get to the bit where you say to her '… When thou holds't up thy hand. O let me kiss this princess of pure white.' Just made for pageantry isn't it?

And Mia is so short and dark in comparison. Just think of the theatricality of it"

"Fantastic."

"What?" This time it was Mia who was uncertain if this was some kind of joke the boys had conjured up. Was something going on between them and Helen that she'd missed out on? But Helen was still looking miserable. Or rather she was looking both miserable and anxious; frightened even.

Helen turned to Mia with reproachful eyes.

"Are you part of this?"

"Part of what?"

"Part of making fun of my height, and everything."

"I could ask you the same—why is everyone making fun of me being short?"

"Girls, girls." Lenny looked exasperated. "No one's making fun of anyone, I just want to make this the greatest show they've ever seen, and Helen is key to this…." He came to a surprised halt as Helen started wailing and crying;

"Stop it. Stop it, all of you."

"Oh for fuck's sake, it's a bloody play we're talking about, not real life," he muttered. "Anyway, I need another drink. I'll go and get a round in. Same again for everyone?" He didn't wait to hear their replies, but hurried back towards the pub.

Dennis turned to Helen, his mind completely on the scene as Lenny had pictured it.

"Come on, let's give it a go. Buck up Helen. Stand tall, and I'll go on one knee—'Lysander, keep thy Hermia, I will none. If e'er I loved her all that love is gone. My heart to her but as a guestwise sojourned, and now to Helena is it home returned. There to remain.'"

He made to grab Helen's hand amorously. She shrieked.

"Don't you dare! Don't you dare make fun of me

under the guise of acting. Mia, how could you let them? You little vixen you! I thought you were my friend, but you're not, you're just a little poison dwarf."

Mia reeled back as if Helen had struck her. Then launched herself at her friend, her nails heading straight towards her face. It took all of Dennis's strength to hold her back. Everyone was relieved when Lenny returned.

"Hey, guys, cool it," he said, looking round at his friends who were all clearly in a heated state.

"I've bought a bottle of wine for you girls—works out cheaper that way than to keep going back and forth buying it by the glass. And Dennis, plenty of ales for you and me. I've blown my week's shopping allowance on this, so you'd all better make it worth my while. Come on, drink up"

Everybody poured themselves a fresh drink, and Mia, knowing that it was far from wise, *not with her head for drink, not in this heat, not on a nearly empty stomach— but what the hell, suddenly it didn't seem the day could get any worse*, drank most of her glass down in one gulp. Lenny then called them to order.

In the distance, but in reality only a few feet from her, Lenny was marshalling the others into action. Mia felt thickheaded and slightly sick. If I just sit down for a minute I might feel better, she thought, and lowered herself gingerly onto the ground. As Lenny passed near her, attempting once more to persuade Helen over something or other—Mia was fast getting beyond caring—a sheet of paper fell from his trouser pocket. Mia leant forward and picked it up.

She knew at once what it was. On the front was a Pre-Raphaelite style picture of a moonlit wood and fairies: a proud Titania, a haughty Oberon, a grinning Puck, sundry other fairies and, to one side, an oafish figure bedecked with flowers and an ass's head. It was the flyer for their performance that night. Lenny must be crazy to be trying to change things so late in the day, she thought, then felt even worse than she'd felt before. *How could she ever think badly of Lenny, her one true love?*

She turned the flyer over and there were all the names of the cast against the characters they were playing in order of appearance. She was third down, followed by the other lovers:

Hermia, in love with Lysander—Mia Cross
Lysander, loved by Hermia—Leonard Barker
Demetrius, suitor of Hermia—Dennis O'Connell
Helena, in love with Demetrius—Helen Dent.

The lovers' misunderstandings are so entertaining on stage and on the page, she thought, even after countless rehearsals. But they're not so funny in real life. She looked over at the others. They were still arguing about this stupid masque idea of Lenny's. *God, had she ever imagined putting the words 'stupid' and 'Lenny' together in the same sentence?* The whole show was going to be a disaster. A nightmare, not a dream.

Helen was crying again, but the boys were comforting her, vying with each other even, to be the most attentive. No, they didn't need her, Mia. Indeed they seemed oblivious to her. This was unsettling and she made a half-hearted attempt to get up and re-join them, but her head started spinning. I'll just rest a bit, she thought, wait till I feel less woozy. I can listen for my cue or they'll call me when they're ready to go on with my bit. She slid back down onto the grass and sighed fretfully. She didn't have the energy for anything else.

It was way too hot for any kind of activity really. Even under the tree canopy, fingers of sun were knifing their way through the spaces between the leaves and scorching her cheeks and shoulders. Without getting up, she shuffled herself towards the base of the largest tree, where there was the most shade available, and settled back down again with her back to the trunk. The bark was rough against her skin, but she couldn't be bothered to move again. *How miserable I am,* she thought, *and how happy I was just a few minutes—or was it hours—or days—or years ago.* Her body was heavy and she felt distinctly weary, but her mind was agitated. *I'm far too upset to sleep,* she thought, *but perhaps if I just try to rest, I will feel a bit better.*

What if I'm too upset to perform tonight, or really ill? Her eyes flew open in alarm a few seconds later. She remembered how she'd chided Helen earlier. How she'd have to act, no matter how miserable she felt. How smug— how crass—it must have sounded. And how much easier it was to dish out advice than receive it, even from oneself. Embarrassed by such thoughts, she closed her eyes again. At first, she listened to the hum of her friends' voices, intermingled with the buzz of a distant bee. Soon the noises were merging together soporifically, and within minutes she was snoring gently.

***

Mia woke with a start. She had no idea how long she had been asleep, but it must have been a few hours as the sun was now firmly to the west and it was cool and pleasant under the trees. She felt thirsty, but certainly didn't want any more wine. Which was just as well because the wine bottle was empty, as were all the beer bottles. *We must have been mad,* she thought, *drinking all that booze just before the show.*

It was completely silent, apart from a distant drone of traffic, and an intermittent murmur of voices from the beer garden. *Where is everybody? Have they left me here alone? What is happening?* She glanced round anxiously and was relieved to see Lenny stretched out to one side of the tree, fast asleep. Slightly further off were Helen and

Dennis. They too were asleep and Dennis had his arm round Helen.

What? Mia sat up, fully awake by now. *What had happened since she had fallen asleep?* She had drifted off to the sound of squabbling and now the estranged lovers were entwined together like the babes in the wood. *How?*

She crawled over to Lenny and poked him gingerly, then stroked his exposed ear lobe to coax him into wakefulness. He groaned and came around reluctantly. But on opening his eyes, and seeing Mia looking down anxiously at him, his face broke into a smile.

"Darling," was all he said as he pulled himself slowly into a sitting position and removed pieces of dried grass and leaf from his dreadlocks. Mia drew back. They had hardly been on close terms when she fell asleep, maybe he was still being provoking.

"How did the rehearsal go?" she asked coolly

Lenny smiled ruefully.

"Madness, complete madness. I don't know what got into me to think we could change things at the last minute. So it's all as we were. At least you don't have to unlearn anything, seeing as you very sensibly nodded off during my idiotic carry-on."

"What about them?" Mia jerked her head towards their two friends.

"Oh, that pair. In their different ways, they made me see sense."

"I mean, them, together…."

Lenny shrugged. "I'm not sure how that happened, but suddenly Dennis accused me of dissing Helen and wanted to fight me over her. I would have laughed if he wasn't so deadly earnest about it. Fortunately, we were both too pissed by that time to throw punches, so we just swore at each other a lot till Helen told us people in the beer garden were starting to look. And now, well, you can see for yourself."

"I'm pleased for Helen, she's been so miserable these past few weeks." She paused. "And us? What about us?"

Lenny gave her his most puckish grin as he stood up and held his hand out to help her up too. "Give me your hands if we be friends…"

"Oh shut up." She giggled happily as she straightened up. "Of course we're friends."

"That's great, because I wanted us to be more than that. You're not still cross with me for getting a bit up myself this afternoon are you? I was terribly drunk, by the end. And now got the thick head to prove it"

"Me too. No, I'm not cross with you. I don't think I could ever be that."

"That's great, because I wanted to ask you something." Lenny went down on bended knee and took her left hand in both his.

"Mia, my dearest, will you marry me?"

Mia's heart took a lurch. Of course she would, sometime, but things were moving a bit too fast for now. Maybe it was only the drink still talking. She pulled him back up and planted a small kiss on his cheek.

"Marry you? Oh Lenny, we hardly know each other yet. Let's wait at least until we're sober, and tonight's performance is over, before thinking about anything so serious."

"The play! I'd forgotten all about that." Lenny clapped his hand to his forehead theatrically, then pulled out his phone. "God. It's five o'clock already. We need to be at the theatre in an hour. And there's a text from my aunt to say she'll be at the stage door at five to six to wish me well. Best wake the others. Oy you two! Helen! Denny!"

He ran over to them as he shouted.

Dennis and Helen woke with a start and, still drowsy, scrambled to their feet. Both remembered at the same time about the play and Helen scrabbled for her phone.

"Don't panic, we've got an hour to get there." Lenny read their thoughts. "Okay, you can panic a little, we'd best not hang about."

"Let's get going then." Dennis took Helen by the hand, and she leant in towards him, as if it were the most natural thing in the world. Mia caught Helen's eye, and smiled.

"Don't ask!" Helen mouthed and smiled back.

"I'm going to have to stop off at the pub loo, before going any further, you lot coming?" Mia asked. Helen and Dennis nodded, and Lenny took Mia by the arm. Despite his support, she swayed a little, then stumbled. Giggling she put on her best Hermia voice and declaimed:

"Methinks I see things with parted eye, when everything seems double."

"That's just the booze talking, you'll see straight soon enough if you put your head under the cold tap when you get to the loo," Lenny said, steering her towards to pub.

"Cheek! I drank far less than the rest of you. And if a cold shower is the order of the day for me, just think what you lot need!"

"Fair enough, it's the cold water treatment for me too," Dennis said. "As for this afternoon—put it down to, oh, I don't know, an attack of midsummer madness."

"I reckon we've all had a bout of that today." Helen hiccupped and grinned. "Along with too much wine and sun."

"Too true." Mia grinned back at her as arm in arm, or hand in hand, the two couples emerged from the wood.

"But that's all behind us for today," Lenny said, quickly. "Soon the sun will be going down, the greasepaint will be going on, and the curtain will be going up for…"

"… *A Midsummer Night's Dream.*" He let the other three finish the sentence for him.

Time Out Of Mind

The Bella Vista is one of the best care homes in northern Italy. It's up in the hills so it's nice and cool and, from the gardens we can look out over the tops of the olive groves, almost down to shores of Lake Garda. The nearest city is Verona, though it's quite a trek to get there; nearly a day on horseback. And jolly sore you'd be by the time you got there, too.

Most of the staff, like me, come from the nearby villages. The residents come from all round, a few are even from the south. I reckon some families must think 'the further away the better' for their elderly loved ones.

I like working here. The pay isn't very good, the shifts are long, and some of the residents are a bit crotchety sometimes. But the work isn't too hard really, most of the ladies are lovely most of the time, and treat you like family. Some of them even think you *are* family! Besides, there's not much else around here for a girl like me, with no education to speak of, and no family money to spare. And the food is really good.

Proper Italian pasta we have, with plenty of fruit and cheese, and the chef bakes all of our bread fresh every day, even on a Sunday. All the residents like the meals, and look forward to lunch and dinner. Once someone bangs the gong there is a mad rush, if you can call it that, when there are crutches, and walking sticks, and arthritic knees involved, to get to the dining room. It's a good job they all have their own special places or there'd be fist fights as they race to get there first, in the hope of getting a bigger helping. When I say 'race' I don't want you to imagine a real race, mind you. Lots of them have wonky hips as well as dodgy knees, so running is out of the question. Even walking fast is beyond them. But a less than dignified kerfuffle takes place as they hurry, after their own fashion, to get to their seats.

Our boss, Maria, decides who sits where when each new resident arrives. She always has two things in mind. First, how nimble is the new person—does it take them forever to get about under their own steam? In which case they can be allocated a place near the door. Or, can they make it on their own to one of the tables further into the room, or with one of us pushing them in a wheelchair? Second, and maybe more important, does the new arrival come from Verona and, if so, what part of the city do they come from? Silly really, but there have been feuds between different areas, and different families from these areas, that go back decades, maybe centuries Even though the council and court have imposed laws and stuff to stop them all having a go at each other, it hasn't stopped it altogether, by a long chalk. Maybe they don't have full blown riots in the street any more, or none that I've heard of anyway, but there's still bad blood and, even in a place like this, tempers fray easily, and crockery is thrown, if you sit people with opposing alliances at the same table. It would be funny if it wasn't so sad to see these old people squabbling away about longstanding grievances over goodness knows what.

Nearly all the residents are female as we rarely have more than three men in here at the same time. Again, it's Maria who decides which of the residents each of us care assistants work with most; who is their 'named carer,' to give us our proper titles. We're supposed to get to know them. You know—find out what their favourite meals are, when (or if) they have family to visit, what they did when they were young—that kind of thing. It makes the job more interesting, and I think the old people like to have someone to take an interest; makes them feel a bit special.

Of course, many of them are really old. A few are still quite independent, but some are in such poor health they need help with washing and dressing, even getting out of their chair and feeding themselves. Quite a few are okay physically, but their minds have gone. They don't know where they are, or even who they are, or who anyone else is. Bit alarming really, I hope I never get like that, but my Nan did. She ended up thinking I was her sister, not her granddaughter, so it's in the family.

"Live long enough to be a nuisance to your children!"

My mum used to say that as a joke when I was still living at home, but when Nan started to wander off all the time, and stopped washing and eating properly, she said it wasn't funny anymore.

The trouble with care homes, at least the good ones like the Bella Vista, is there's always a waiting list. So a new resident has to wait for someone to die before they can move in. And that can be really upsetting, especially when that person had been here for years and you've grown fond of them, and think they have been fond of you, too. One day they're in their usual chair, hoping you've got time for a chat. Next day they're gone and there's another little old lady sitting in there, and you have to welcome her, and make her feel like it's her home now, and that she'll be happy at the Bella Vista. You have to make her feel safe, and take an interest in her ailments and her hobbies, if she has any. But, all the time, you're feeling miserable because the last old lady sitting in that chair had become a special friend, almost like another Nan, and you still hadn't heard all her life history or got to the bottom of those events in her life that had been so important to her once.

Nursey was like that. She had a proper name of course, but no-one ever called her by it.

"Just call me Nurse, love, like everybody else does," she begged us all, even the boss, when she first arrived and we asked her if she wanted us to call her by her first name, or would she prefer to be known as Mrs -.

"Nurse is just fine," she said. "I won't know who

you mean if you call me anything else."

So we called her Nursey, not to confuse her with the real nurses in the infirmary. She was one of my special ladies. She was very unhappy, and cried a lot, when she first arrived. I thought she was a bit muddle-headed, to be honest, as she said everything at least twice. Very nosey she was too, always asking about my family and my love life—but in such a friendly way, I never took offence.

Nursey often talked about her daughter, who she called Susan, and then she would talk about her young mistress who she looked after. But when I asked her "Do you mean it was Susan you were looking after?" she looked at me astonished, and said "No, no. Susan, bless her little heart, joined the angels when she was still a baby."

Her records said she was a widow and had no children. Certainly no one came to see her, except very early on when a priest, or something, came one afternoon, and they'd sat and cried together about the young mistress and her boy husband and how things were supposed to have got better in Verona, but the families never recovered, and Nursey wouldn't be here if it had never happened—her young mistress would have seen to that. I thought, perhaps, the priest (except he wasn't a priest, but a friar, as I found out later) was a little funny in the head too, as he seemed to agree with her story, and kept saying her husband would have been a lovely master. *So, was she talking about her daughter? Who died in infancy? In which case how could she have had a husband? Or was it her own husband?*

Like I said, the friar was very old, but perhaps he was just going along with her to humour her. Anyway, he never came again. Maybe he died, or found the journey up from Verona too much for his old bones. But Nursey often talked about him and his skill in making medicines to help people. Then again, she talked about him making poisons that killed people. Confused? I certainly was after talking to her some days!

And Nursey could talk. Quite saucy she was too, on times. Once she was talking about Susan—by this time I was clear that she really had once had a daughter called Susan. One day, Nursey said, the little girl had tripped and fallen flat on her face and her husband had picked her up and said she would be falling flat on her back soon enough with the right man around. I didn't understand what she was on about. Then she made this gesture with her finger and wiggled her hips. It only took me a couple of seconds then to work out what she meant, and I could feel myself blushing. Really! I didn't think people thought about such things at her age, let alone talked about them.

She chuckled when she saw my red face, and said her old mistress hadn't approved either when she'd told her about it, and her young mistress had told her to shut up too when she came in. Then, she and her mother started talking about her getting married soon. That is, her young mistress getting married, not her daughter. So she hadn't been talking about Susan after all.

After this, she went all sad again, and mopped her eyes and mumbled about Susan and her young mistress being the same age and both gone before their time, and her now a feeble old woman, no use to anyone. And I wasn't sure what to say, especially as I wasn't sure who she meant by her 'old' as well as her 'young' mistress. But, thankfully, the gong for dinner sounded, and Nursey perked up right away. I helped her up, she gathered her sticks together and scuttled off to her allotted seat in the dining room.

Nursey was from Verona. Maria thought a lot about where she should sit, and decided to put her on one of the near tables with three elderly widows from the surrounding villages so as not to cause trouble with any of the other Veronese ladies. But it was hard to see Nursey hurting a fly, let alone playing a part in any big feud, although she might upset her fellow diners with her dirty jokes. Perhaps they think talking about things like that is okay in the city, but women from the villages certainly don't, not if my Nan was anything to go by.

***

One day, just to try and find out a bit more about Nursey and her life before she came into the Bella Vista, I asked her about the friar who'd been to see her soon after she first arrived, and how she came to know him. At first she didn't seem to know who I meant.

"You know," I prompted her. "The old man who makes medicines... or is it poisons... to help people. He came to visit you once when you first came here."

"Ah," she said after a long pause. "Friar Lucio. We go back a long way. No, no, not Lucio. Oh dear, what's the matter with my memory these days, no one ever calls a Friar 'Lucio' do they? It doesn't sound holy enough does it, dear? But it was something like that. Began with 'L' that's for certain."

"Leo?" I said, "Louis? Luigi?" She shook her head at all of these. I was running out of men's names beginning with 'L', but then I remembered my mother's second cousin by marriage. "Laurence?"

"That's it," she cried, delightedly. "Friar Laurence. What a dear, dear, man. He lived in a cave you know. Well, not a cave exactly, more a hermit's cell. Yes, a snug little cell in the woods just outside the city walls. Always the smell of herbs drying....." She drifted off into a reverie at the remembrance of the holy man's living accommodation, but I was impatient to know more.

"Yes, very nice," I said. "But how did you come to know him?"

She didn't answer me directly, and I was just going to prompt her again, when she smiled sadly and murmured.

"So kind, when my Susan died, and then my husband. And he meant kindly, too, when he gave them poison."

"What?" I exclaimed. "He poisoned your daughter and husband?"

She looked at me with clouded, troubled eyes.

"Who, dear?"

"Friar Laurence. He poisoned your husband and daughter?"

"Of course not, whatever gave you that idea?"

I was about to say—"well, you did"—but she'd closed her eyes and fallen into a doze. I shook her gently by the shoulder, but it was too late and, anyway, Maria was beckoning me to go and run an errand for her. So I left Nursey dozing peacefully. But my interest had been well caught. I knew what I wanted to talk about with Nursey again tomorrow!

Nursey fell sick in the night, and spent over a month with the nurses in the infirmary, so I didn't get the chance to speak to her straight away. When she came back she was much frailer, and needed my help to wash and dress in the morning. She was quite exhausted when all this was over, and sat down in her favourite chair with a sigh, and closed her eyes. But not for long. Soon, she opened them again, looked straight at me and smiled.

"It's so nice to be back," she said, contentedly. "And you are just as kind and thoughtful as the last girl. You must tell me all about yourself."

"But I am the same girl, Nursey—don't you recognise me? It's me, Clara."

A worried look came over her face, and she peered at me closely. Then she smiled anxiously.

"Of course you are, dear. Clara, of course. Just my silly brain." She paused, and wrung her hands a bit, before looking at me again. "Remind me, dear, why am I here with you, and not with my young mistress?"

I took both her hands. "You started to get old, and there was no one to look after you, so you came here. A friar—Friar Laurence—he helped organise it, I think, on account of your daughter, or your young mistress, being dead."

She was looking down at her lap, at her gnarled old hands in my smooth young ones, and nodding vaguely as I spoke, but lifted her head properly when I mentioned the friar's name."

"Poor Friar Laurence," she said, after a bit. "And he meant so well. He didn't want anyone to die, he wanted them to live and stop the killing. But they died, poor lambs."

"Who? How did they die, Nursey?" She was gazing sadly into the distance, remembering things from her past, oblivious of me. I knew I mustn't rush her but I thought I would go mad with curiosity if she didn't tell me more. I let go of her hands, and stroked her cheek, till she looked back at me. Slowly, her eyes re-focused on me and she smiled brightly.

"Ah, Jules," she said. "I'd forgotten you were here."

"Not Jules, Clara. There's no one called Jules here. Tell me Nursey—who died? And did Friar Laurence kill them?"

"He killed her so she could live. Such a clever plan. But there was a plague in Mantua, so they all died."

Nursey had me really confused now. I knew for sure she was from Verona, so where did Mantua come into it? I was about to ask her some more questions, but her chin had fallen onto her chest, and she was snoring gently. Poor Nursey, she looked so shrunken and fragile, sitting there. I felt bad then, and worried that I had tired her out. Usually, she loved to talk. But I still had no idea how much of what she was saying was true, and how much was fantasy. And I did so want to know. Instead, I tucked a rug round her gently, so as not to wake her, and went off to see to one of my other ladies.

Nursey was brighter the next day. She greeted me

with my proper name and asked several times after my family and whether I had a boyfriend yet. As usual, when I said no, she reminded me that, at seventeen, I was leaving it a bit late and I would be left on the shelf if I wasn't careful. This time she added a bit more information from her own life without me prompting. Her old mistress, she said, had been married and given birth to her young mistress before she was fifteen and her young mistress had nearly been married twice before she was fourteen.

"Really?" I asked. It wasn't unknown for high born girls from the city to marry young, but two husbands at thirteen was a bit out of the ordinary, even for them. "Did the first one die young?"

"Oh, yes," she replied. "But that wasn't the reason. He killed her cousin, you see, so Friar Laurence thought it would be best to pretend she was dead too so she wouldn't have to marry the other one."

Friar Laurence again. *Did he really come up with so many cunning plans, or was Nursey completely muddled?* Nursey could see I didn't really believe her, and she became quite agitated. But she was obviously upset, too, about the fate of her young mistress.

"He married them, but then, when he killed her cousin, he had to flee to Mantua, so my old mistress and master thought she wouldn't pine for her cousin if she were married. I thought so too, but she was having none of it. She was very cross with me about that, poor lamb, although she pretended not to be."

"But how could her parents allow her to marry again when she was already married?"

"Only Friar Laurence and I knew about the first one. Love at first sight it was. So quick! So Friar Laurence married them before—you know." She smiled knowingly and winked. "Anyway, he thought the families would be reconciled, with the two lovers married, and there would be peace on the streets of Verona. But then he killed her cousin and had to flee, so I couldn't see why she shouldn't marry the one her parents wanted for her all along. He was as rich and handsome as the first. And lusty too, by the look of him; he'd have taken her mind off grieving for the other one. So why not?"

I could see lots of reasons why not, but couldn't work out whether Nursey had got the story all wrong, the dates all wrong, or really was unable to see there was a problem with keeping the first marriage a secret. And there was one thing I felt sure about Nursey and secrets—she wouldn't have been very good at keeping this one!

"But surely Friar Laurence wouldn't marry them when he knew her first husband was still alive?"

"He took poison and died when he heard she was dead. But she only took poison to pretend to be dead to avoid marrying the other one. But, when she saw he was dead, she killed herself."

This was sounding more and more unlikely.

"How could she see he was dead, Nursey. Hadn't he fled to Mantua?"

"They were both dead, side by side. I saw them." Nursey was angry that I was doubting her word. "Dead, both of them," she repeated loudly, and I was worried she was upsetting some of the other residents. Suddenly, she started to shake and pant and her lips turned blue. Hastily, I called out for help and Maria and two care assistants rushed in. Between us we helped Nursey into a wheelchair and, on Maria's instructions, took her straight to the infirmary.

She mumbled to herself, as we wheeled her quickly down the corridor. I was feeling so guilty, believing it was my fault that she was in such an agitated state but, as we reached the ward and were about to hand her over to the nurses, she clutched my hand.

"You're a sweet girl, Jules," she said, softly. "If you'd lived, I would have minded your babies too. I would have been wanted, and I wouldn't have come to a place like this. But then," she looked straight at me, and I could almost hear the switches in her brain re-connecting. "I would never have met you, Clara. And no one else is interested in a poor old woman like me anymore."

***

Nursey died in the night. Within two days there was another old lady sitting in her chair. A grumpy old thing from one of the nearby villages, who didn't seem to have done anything of interest in all her eighty odd years on this earth. It was hard to feel any real concern for her as she answered all my attempts to talk to her about her health, or her family, or what she'd like to do today, with a grunt or a sniff. But at least her refusal to do or say anything, gave me plenty of time to daydream, and think about the past occupant of this chair, who had been so full of life and gossip.

I often puzzled over the things that Nursey had told me, and what bits were true, and what was just part of her muddled thinking. Eventually, though, there was more and more work to do with several new residents arriving all at once, so those long chats with Nursey just became a fond memory. Oh, and I had at last found myself a boyfriend. Nursey would have been pleased. And relieved for, as she would have kept saying if she were still here, my shelf life was fast running out.

One evening, said new boyfriend told me a troupe of actors from Verona were putting on a play in the village square. It was my evening off and we didn't have anything better to do so we went to see it. It was written by some English bloke whose name I forget now. All about a girl and boy falling madly in love, two feuding families, a gossipy old nanny, and an elderly friar. Lots of fights, or people trying to stop the fights, and it ended with nearly all the young people dead. My hankie was sopping by the end, it was so sad. At the same time, the plot sounded cosily familiar.

Dear Nursey, had she been to see this play one time in Verona before she came to the Bella Vista? She was such an old romantic, I can see why she would have loved the story. And I'm sure that is far more likely than that some English chap had written a play about how she and an elderly friar had tried to help two star crossed lovers get together. Maybe, as old age had worn away her wits, his tragic love story had become more real to her than her own life? After all, if I remember right, someone says at the end of the play – "they don't come much fuller of tragedy and of woe, than this one of Juliet and her Romeo."

The Quality of Mirth

Tuesday

Dear Diary,

Well, I haven't had a chance to write much in you recently. It's just been *sooo* busy, what with the old master dying, the funeral, and stuff. Then the lawyers read out the will. All to go to his only daughter Portia, my mistress, as was expected. But the crafty old goat has tied it up in such a way that it depends on who she marries whether she gets anything. Or nothing. Did I say crafty? Cruel more like. What if my poor mistress ends up having to marry someone she doesn't like, or hasn't met before? When I just *know* she already fancies someone else rotten.

Yes, I know she's lost her heart to some Venetian lord. But he hasn't any money, probably not even enough to come courting her when he hears about the contest. And one thing is certain, she's not going to be short of suitors. It's well-known the old boy has left quite a bit. Oh, I know I shouldn't talk about him like that. It's disrespectful, but, I mean, come on! This is the sixteenth century after all, and it's as if he's put his daughter up for auction!

She's not a bit pleased about it, I can tell. But she has always been a dutiful daughter; at least, she has never openly defied him. Now she just shrugs, and says her father was only doing what he thought was best for her, and she'll go along with it, whatever. But as you know, dear Diary, my happiness is tied up with hers. There's only one choice she can make that will suit both of us and, at the moment, that seems as likely as snow in June. So we're both a bit miserable at the moment. *Sigh*!

Thing is, the old master has set a test for all potential suitors. Three caskets, one gold, one silver, and one lead. Inside one of them is a picture of my mistress and his permission for the finder to marry his daughter and take all his wealth. Pick the wrong one though and the unlucky fellow has to promise never to marry anyone. That's right, a life of celibacy for the hapless suitor. So, unless lover-boy Bassanio, for that's his name, arrives from Venice in time, *and* picks the right cask, it'll be a life of misery for my mistress. And for me too, as I am sticking with her come what (or rather who) may. Yikes, I could end up dying an old maid.

The chance of scooping up a fortune has had them all running here. Princes and other nobles from around Italy, the Palatine, France, Scotland, England and Germany. Luckily, my mistress hasn't had to worry about any of that lot. As soon as they heard the price of picking the wrong casket, to a man, they stared down at their cod-pieces, hemmed and hawed a bit, and decided that her great fortune simply wasn't worth the risk. And now they've all packed their bags and gone back to where they came from— hooray!

But that still left the Princes of Morocco and Aragon, who arrived as the other lot were going. Seems this pair were willing to chance their arm to get their hands on the money, and on my mistress, of course. She's gorgeous to look at, and no side to her, a truly kind and generous mistress. I'm not fooled for a minute that that's really why they're here, when so much money is at stake. Oh, and she's also clever. Very. And that often puts men off. So, *nooo*; they're not here for her wise views either.

What hardly anyone knows, apart from me, and you of course, dear Diary, as I tell you everything, is what fun she is. All that cleverness isn't just poring over books— though she does a fair amount of that—Latin, Greek, philosophy, law, even medicine; and I wish she wouldn't tell me all the gory bits about losing limbs, and blood, and stuff, as it makes me queasy. But then, she only does that as a joke to make me turn green, and maybe go faint. Then she'll laugh, bring me round with her smelling salts and say "Enough, of that. Time for some proper fun!" and we'll have a good giggle over some saucy rhymes she's found that I'm sure well brought up girls like her shouldn't understand. Or, we'll laugh about some of the sillier men who used to hang round the place when her father was alive, hoping to get permission to woo her.

Sometimes, we'll set off for a day in the country, just the two of us, to see her cousin who is as clever as she is, and doesn't mind it that it is a woman he is pitting his wits against. She can hold her end up in an argument, and he seems to like that. Oh, they'll talk about anything, politics and philosophy mostly. But sometimes they discuss legal matters though they often lose me at the first 'point of order.' So much law seems to be in Latin too, so really I'm lost before I start. Portia has taught me many things. That's the wonderfulness of working for her, she treats me more like a fellow student than a maid. But she's never got round to teaching me Latin. And am I glad of that, too! Writing and speaking my own language is hard enough, never mind getting into dead grammar constructions only clever people have bothered with for hundreds of years. I don't see much point in learning it myself—though I suppose people like lawyers and doctors need to know such stuff, or they'd be out of business.

Her father didn't like her travelling alone (even when I was with her—a maid doesn't count, I suppose). But he let her visit her cousin whenever she wanted to. Nowhere else mind, unless he or a manservant came too. But sometimes, when he was busy, or out of town, or had taken to his sick-bed, she and I dressed up as young men and set off, all man-like, into the town to wander through the market place and watch the townsfolk going about their business. What wonderful freedom the blokes have, just to come and go as they please. And to wear a doublet and hose they can properly stride about in, rather than a stupid gown that trails in the mud or dust, and nips you in so tight at the waist you can hardly breathe, and makes you go faint if you try to walk fast or run. And even the smallest breasted girl ends up with quite a 'come hither' bosom on show with those bustier things. No, you don't really feel safe going out on your own as a woman, what with all the men, even the meanest servant, leering down the front of your dress. And don't mention the silly shoes women are supposed to wear. Give me a man's low heeled footwear any time!

So it's good to go out as a man, and put yourself about with no one staring. And I'm not telling anyone, only you dear Diary, but I do rather fancy myself in breeches and leather boots. Sometimes I wish I'd been born a boy. But then I wouldn't have been employed to wait on my mistress. And I just love her—would follow her to the ends of the earth, as they say. Especially if it means I can also dress up as a boy from time to time!

Anyway, darling Diary, my candle is nearly spent and I'm finding it hard to keep my eyes open, so back to the two remaining princes and what happened to them before I tumble into bed. Well they picked the wrong caskets! Naturally they went for the most expensive ones. But the old master hadn't put his daughter's picture in either of them. So they too have packed their bags and gone off for a life of single beds and bachelor pursuits. Ha, ha! I'm a bit sorry for them, really, but not sorry enough that I haven't thanked God on bended knees for my mistress's sake, for their mistakes. Neither were her type at all, and as for their menservants - *meh!*

So I'm off to bed now with a hopeful heart. There's still time for Bassanio to turn up with the gorgeous Gratanio in tow. Just think if he arrives soon and picks the right box! Oh, if only we could let him know which ones have been chosen already without success, but my mistress has been expressly forbidden to give any indication. Maybe he'll know by instinct, after all he's really poor, yet he knows my mistress loves him. So he knows that wealth isn't a big thing for her. That's a fine sentiment when you've already got plenty, I know, but all that glisters is not gold, or whatever. Oh if only he can get it right—then it's both me and my mistress sorted, if I'm a judge of his manservant's inclinations. And I am! I am!

Oh, bother. The candle really is spluttering now. Only a few seconds left. I must leave you now Diary dear. And pray in the dark for the arrival of two handsome Venetians and the happiest of outcomes for me and my mistress.

***

Thursday

Dear Diary,

Yes! Yes! Yes!

It's all working out just brill, which is why I didn't have time to write in you yesterday. Bassanio and Gratiano arrived, and my mistress did her best to keep her composure. But she couldn't conceal her love for him for long. She tried to stop him opening any casket at all for as long as she could. I know she was afraid that if he opened the wrong one she would never see him again, and she didn't want to face that. Better to live for the moment, and at least have a few happy memories, I suppose.

Her plan worked for a bit, which was good as it gave me and Gratiano a bit more time to get to know each other. Not like that, you saucy thing. I blush to write in you, if you're going to think that way! But you're on the right track; we do want to, and so much of our future happiness depends on his master choosing wisely. So we didn't want to push the matter either; we would wait on events as his master and my mistress dilly-dallied. However, Bassanio said he couldn't stay very long as a friend was depending on his swift return. He had to make his choice that day and know, one way or another, what his fate might be. So off we all went to the little chamber where all the caskets were laid out.

He took his time then, I can tell you, wandering round and looking at each of them and muttering to himself. My mistress stood as impassive as she could by the doorway, but I could see that she was trembling, and her cheeks were sometimes flushed and sometimes pale. I tried to catch Bassanio's eye and then stare meaningfully at the lead casket, to give him a bit of a clue. But he never looked in my direction. I carried on staring at the lead one, however, in the hope that just willing him to pick it might work.

Dear God, he didn't half take his time but, in the end, he stopped dead still in front of the lead casket. Maybe he could feel my eyes boring into him then, as he looked round quickly, before placing his hand firmly on the lid and declaring he had made his choice.

He opened it, peered in and let out a *whoop!* Well he was a bit more dignified than that—it was probably me who whooped, truth to tell. He put his hand inside and pulled out a portrait of Portia. Then they fell into each other's arms and just snogged forever. Gratiano rushed over to me and we started snogging too. Eventually my mistress looked up. I think she was a bit surprised to see me at it with her lover's man, and Bassanio did a double take too when he came up for air. They had been so wrapped up in their own passion, they hadn't noticed the growing *tendresse* between their respective servants. See, my mistress has taught me a bit of French, if not any Latin, *tant mieux*. But they were fine with it. We had a good laugh, and they agreed to us marrying at the same time as them.

It should have all been such fun time, with a honeymoon, if only a very short one, for both couples. But it was all cut short by a message from Venice for Bassanio to return AT ONCE! Seems this friend of his had lent him money to court my mistress, as he'd anticipated big profits on his overseas trading deals. But these had all gone belly up, and Bassanio was needed back in Venice to try and sort things out with a rogue of a money lender, who was out for his friend's life.

He had to go. Of course he had to go. Portia could see that, and she was happy for him to use her money to help in any way it could. But first she wanted to be married. So, a quick ceremony for both of us, a short, sleepless, night, Diary, I'm too modest to tell you more, then we were up out of bed to see our husbands off. But not before each of us gave them a ring from our own fair fingers which, we told them, if they were truly loyal to their new and loving, and enduringly faithful, wives, they would never part with. Of course they promised they would rather die than part with these rings. We bid them farewell, and my mistress and I went back indoors to catch up on our sleep.

Well, that's what I thought we would be doing. But Portia had other ideas. She's calling me now to get things ready. Ready for what you're asking, but no time to write more. I'll fill you in when I get another moment.

***

Friday.

Dear Diary,

Here I am again, but this really is going to be a quick entry. I just love my mistress, can't imagine working for anyone else, they'd be so *boorinnnng....*

The things she thinks of, well they just make your

hair stand on end! You'd never guess, but she's decided on us following our husbands to Venice. She loves Bassanio, and would go to the end of the earth for him. But she understands his limitations too, and she knows she's cleverer than he is. At least I think that's what she thinks. She hasn't said so in so many words. But what she has said leads me to believe that she knows, with her learning, she will have a better chance of saving his friend than he will.

"But, how madam?" I asked her. After all, as far as I knew from what we told our husbands, we were going to wait here quietly till they returned. But no. She has told the household that the pair of us are going away, to a nunnery or something, whilst our menfolk are absent. What we are really doing is heading as fast as we can to her cousin's place, where she will pick his brains and gather up some legal books. Then we're hot footing it to Venice to act as lawyer and clerk for Bassanio's friend. Seems those long, legal chats and arguments she and her cousin indulged in haven't been such a waste of time after all!

"Just one problem, madam," I said to her. "It doesn't matter how wise you are in matters of law, we are women, and no one is going to listen to us, or even let us anywhere near a court."

Portia winked at me. "No problem, my dear Nerissa. My cousin has clothes to spare, as well as law books." Her plan is that we go disguised as young men. An earnest lawyer and his clerk, both of us steeped in knowledge of the law. What a lark! But deadly serious, too. Portia made that clear to me; a man's life may depend on her.

I became all serious too, and a bit worried. It was one thing to strut around the local town in breeches, pretending to be a young man, but how would we pass ourselves off in a court? My mistress, however, is nothing if not confident about our disguises, and her ability. Anyway, she added, less encouragingly, she's sure we won't have any problem convincing them to listen to us, as they're likely to be desperate for help by the time we arrive. To convince them, if they needed convincing, she would mention her cousin's name and say we came from him. That he is a celebrated lawyer, and we come with his blessing, should re-assure them about us, despite our seeming youth. Let us hope so, they're bound to notice our voices haven't even broken, for heaven's sake!

"And then, when we've won the case, which we will, don't you worry about that, my little maid, we will have some fun."

She was laughing again now and started dancing around as I chased after her begging her to tell me how we it was possible to have fun whilst being sober and sensible lawyers.

"Well," she said, her eyes twinkling. "Being as they'll both be so grateful to us for saving their friend's life, I'm sure they will offer to do anything for us, or give us anything. So I'm going to get Bassanio to give me the ring I gave him and which he swore he'd never part with."

"He wouldn't. Not since he promised you he wouldn't."

Portia tapped the side of her nose, and smiled knowingly.

"If I have learnt anything about the strength of male friendship, he will," she replied.

"Then I'll do the same with Gratiano." I cried, getting into the spirit of the thing.

"Good for you! But we have to race back here ahead of them, once we have the rings, and change into our dresses. As soon as we hear them arriving, we'll rush out to greet them and take them by the hand. Then scold them soundly for losing our rings so quickly!"

"Mistress, you're a genius!" We both started giggling madly, dancing round the courtyard with our hands clapped to our mouths, as if to contain these wicked plans inside us. Suddenly my mistress stopped, looked at the sundial and declared,

"Enough! We've lots to do and no time to waste. Get your bags, we must be off in two ticks."

And so, dear Diary, I must stop now. We have a great task in hand, and not a second to waste. Wish us luck!

Journey to the Fair Mountain

We were so cold when we arrived. My hands and feet were numb, my nose felt raw and my cheeks were stinging. I could feel my hair, damp and icy, clinging round my face and neck. Alise, with blue lips and streaming eyes, stumbled as she helped me down from my horse. She arranged my gown whilst the old retainer, who had accompanied us on the last part of the journey, dismounted stiffly and knocked on the great door. The rest of the retinue melted away into other parts of the castle, taking the horses with them. The clip-clop of their hooves on the cobbles created a ghostly echo that lingered in the chill air. Alise pushed my hair back from my face and patted my shoulder gently.

"You look lovely, milady," she said, encouragingly.

The door was opened by a young man, who took my hand and drew me quickly into the great hall. Alise followed, as did the old man who bowed deeply to the younger man then settled into the background, his cloak merging with the tapestries on the walls.

He was younger than I had expected, about twenty-five, not that much older than I was. But his manner was so much more assured. Tall and handsome; his thick, black hair fell about his shoulders in gentle waves. He had deep blue eyes and gave me a lingering smile as he held my hand. I felt a tremor pass through me that was more than just the cold. He held my hand tighter and put it to his lips, but the trembling did not stop, even as I curtseyed.

"Your hand is frozen," he said, stroking it gently, and looking straight into my eyes. "It must have been a hard journey through the snow."

I nodded, and bit my lip to stop it quivering as I lowered my eyes, shy and awkward under his probing gaze, too awed to say we had had no snow that day.

Was this the one? My future husband? And was it really less than a week since I left my own home? It felt such a long, long time ago.

***

December 13th was the day my life changed forever. People had not celebrated Saint Lucia's day in the duchy before my mother arrived. It was one of the few Swedish customs she had clung to, and one my father had always indulged her in. So, now it was an annual fixture in the calendar, at least in our part of the kingdom. And many of the girls and young women around me looked forward to it.

I had mixed feelings. Yes, it was exciting to dress up in a white velvet gown and a lovely red sash. On crisp starlit nights I used to enjoy the procession from the castle, round the village and into the little church for a small service with lots of singing, not too much praying, and no sermon to speak of. Then home by the quickest route for warm drinks and freshly made saffron buns. And dancing! I loved the dancing. It marked the start of the Christmas festivities.

But I couldn't help feeling for the suffering the actual Lucia endured to become a martyr, and then a saint. After all, the candles that twinkled so magically in our hands, as we paraded through the village in the gathering darkness, represented the fire her persecutors used, to try to burn her to death when their other cruel efforts failed.

For the last couple of years I, as the oldest daughter of the house—and the duke's daughter at that—had been expected to lead the procession, and then be the hostess for the evening celebrations. My father may have had the smallest dukedom in Denmark, little more than one large island, and three much smaller ones, close to the Swedish mainland, but my mother was keen for me to learn to be a proper lady, maybe another duke's wife one day. I was, by nature, reticent. I felt awkward in the company of young men apart from my dear twin, Rufus, and his friends, and I hated it when she talked like that. I loathed being the center of attention at any type of gathering.

When I had to lead the procession the year before, at least Rufus had been there in the church to meet me and later, laughing and joking—and eating far more than his fair share of saffron buns—he was at my side to greet people for the supper. But this year he decided to go hunting with his friends, so wouldn't be back till much later. How I wished I could have gone with him!

Instead, I was on my own to lead the procession, wearing a crown of whortleberry twigs and nine candles. The crown was lovely to look at, but it hurt my temples where the twigs dug in. After a while, as I knew from last year, the candles would make my head too hot, and my cheeks would go pink from the heat of the flames, despite the cold night air. Worse, the candles would light up my face to reveal my discomfort to all the world. Later, without my crown, and trying not to be too tongue-tied, I would have to welcome the other girls and their families back to the castle for supper, and do my best to ensure that they, at least, were enjoying themselves.

Of course my small sisters would be there, as all four of them were old enough now to take part in the procession and attend the supper. But they were not yet old enough to be a source of support. Not like Rufus who, with his rough and ready humour, could tease me into acting much more boldly that I actually felt. My mother was just impatient with me.

"High time you grew up and accepted your responsibilities. You're a woman now, not a little girl. You will have to do a lot more than this when you are married," was all she said when I begged her to find someone else to take the leading role.

I didn't want to think of marrying, not for years

anyway and, until then, I was happy to be in the background. Let Rufus shine. He was born to be a leader, and would make an excellent duke when the time came. He knew what the future held for him and was comfortable with it. In fact, because of my father's growing ill health, he was already taking on some of his responsibilities. Maybe, I wondered hopefully, I could stay on at the castle when he became the duke and help to run his household ….

When Rufus set off that morning into the crisp winter air, my mother made him promise to be careful, and to be back for supper. He solemnly gave her his word, and vowed he would bring back a boar, maybe two, for the feast on Christmas day. And then he was off, waving cheerfully and blowing me a kiss.

"See you soon, Sis, you'll be just fine!" were his last words to me as his lively horse danced on the on the frozen earth, and tossed her head up and down, eager to be off.

I didn't see him alive again. He fell from his horse as he closed in on a boar— the biggest in the forest, it was said—and was trampled to death. His maimed and bloodied body was brought home by his friends and laid on the floor of the great hall, bringing the St Lucia's day supper to an abrupt end.

My father had been in poor health for some time, but it was the sudden death of his son and heir that brought on his final decline. He survived the winter and, against all expectation, clung on to life through the spring, summer, and into the autumn. But the doctors were convinced he could not survive another winter and urged him to make known his plans for the duchy and his remaining family.

What had been working out as a measured handover of powers from one generation to the next had been thrown into chaos by my brother's death, and even I could see that my father was not really capable of making decisions, though my mother, strong, capable and loyal as she was, did her best to help him. In the short term, the stewards could run the estate, and oversee the tenant farmers but, on my father's death, the land and title was due to pass to a distant cousin whom I had never seen and who had never set foot on this island. *How, my father wondered fretfully, could he be sure that his widow and five daughters would be adequately looked after when he was gone?* But he came to no decision. Instead, an uneasy inertia hung over the household, as we waited for him to die.

A month after my brother's death, this cousin sent his condolences. Recently widowed himself, he wrote he could understand the pain we were experiencing. My mother read the letter with disdain and didn't even bother to show it to my father. For years she had hated this cousin, with increasing vehemence, for the threat he posed to her family's stability. Despite numerous pregnancies, she had failed to produce more than one male heir—my dear Rufus, now dead.

Later in the year, just as autumn had turned to winter and we were experiencing the first frosty nights of late November, this cousin wrote again. My mother was incensed, as I knew she would be, when his letter arrived. She assumed he was writing with tactless haste to remind my father of his inheritance. In fact, as she read the letter, she appeared strangely moved by its contents. As before, it was addressed to my father, but she had started to read it out loud in front of my sisters and me. She suddenly stopped and continued in silence, quashing our pleas for her to continue with a stern "Shh."

When she finished she folded the letter, tapped it thoughtfully with her finger, smiled to herself, and went straight into my father's bedchamber without another word to us. She spent almost an hour closeted with him, and emerged red-eyed, but purposeful. Catching sight of me playing listlessly with one of the house dogs in the hall outside, she spoke sharply.

"Haven't you got better things to do, my girl?"

Then her voice softened.

"You must go into your father now; he wants to see you." She kissed me on the forehead with unusual tenderness and ushered me firmly towards the door.

I knocked the door softly and heard my father's weak voice summon me in. The room was hot and reeked of sickness. I stood in the doorway and curtseyed, reluctant to go further into the stench, but my father raised his hand and beckoned me to him. I had no option but to advance and kneel by his bedside. He put a cold, thin hand on the top of my head. When he spoke his breath was laboured, each word struggling to get out.

"Dearest daughter, you know that I am dying." I raised my head to protest, but he stayed me with his hand. "No, no time for protest. Too tired." He paused to regain his strength, his lungs heaving to take in enough breath to continue. "My esteemed cousin, my heir, has written. He is, as you know, a widower. He has offered his hand in marriage to my oldest daughter."

I gasped. I had no wish to marry, even though I was nearly seventeen. *Surely he understood that?* My father saw the alarm in my eyes.

"It will secure this castle as a home for your mother and sisters," he said. "And you will become the queen."

I shook my head. Please, not marriage to some old man, possibly sick and shriveled and smelly like my father. Weakly, my father took my hand in his dry and bony one. I tried not to recoil.

"My cousin is still young," he said gently, as if he could read my thoughts. "Many say that he is handsome."

I felt ashamed of my selfishness. He squeezed my hand, though the pressure was almost non-existent.

"You will do this for your mother and sisters? Respect my dying wish?"

"Oh, Father," I cried, taking both his wafer thin

hands in mine. And on this my mother entered—she must have been listening at the door—and kissed me. Together we watched my father take his last few breaths. Then she closed his eyelids, pulled the sheet up over his face, and called the servants to damp down the fire and bring fresh rushes for the floor.

My mother replied to the letter on my father's behalf, informing our cousin of his new inheritance, and of the acceptance of his proposal of marriage to me. I was to be dispatched at once, to avoid the worst of the winter weather. A trusted lady-in-waiting would accompany me as my mother could not leave my younger sisters. She, my mother, would sort a suitable trousseau for me, and that would follow in the spring.

I could not help thinking that such haste was unnecessary, driven only by my mother's fear our cousin might change his mind about the marriage offer. But she was fierce and determined, masking any grief and anxiety she might be feeling with restless activity, and putting all her energy into organising my departure. There was no arguing with her.

Alise wasn't really a lady-in-waiting; only my mother had one of those, and she was too old and too arthritic for such a journey. Besides, Gerthe would have been distressed at parting with my mother whom she had first nursed as a baby. Instead my mother selected one of the daughters of the chief steward—a large, jolly young woman, who was a little older than I was. She was keen to see the wider world beyond the dukedom and would, my mother thought, be a sturdy and sensible companion for me on the journey and beyond. I wasn't so sure. We seemed so different—she was by nature cheerful and chatty, while I was quiet and dreamy. But her optimism about her new life was infectious, if only a little. It helped me bear the sadness of my father's funeral, following so soon after my dear brother's, even though my mother, ever thrifty, arranged for the simple meal afterwards to serve as the occasion for the family and servants to bid me farewell.

I set off the next day, on Maise, my favourite horse. I cried hard before I mounted, as did my sisters, and even my mother shed a tear as she kissed me on the forehead, then hugged me briefly to her bosom.

"Be brave, my dearest one," she murmured. "It will be strange at first. It was strange for me too when I came here to be married to your father. And I was barely fifteen. But he was a good man, and you are to marry a good man, too."

I couldn't help remembering that this was not what she had always called her cousin-in-law. I just hoped she was right this time, though the thought made me cry harder. Then she chided me briskly, helped me mount my horse, and made me promise to send word as soon as I had arrived safely.

Alise, meanwhile, bid a tearful farewell to her father and the rest of her family but, at my mother's call, she jumped onto her waiting horse and pulled up alongside me with a bright smile. Two of the male servants then came on horseback to escort us down to the little harbour where a boat was waiting to take us to the mainland, and two others fell in behind, bringing a trunk of clothing for the journey.

There was no real bond between Alise and me, and for much of the way to the harbour we traveled in silence. I was nursing in private my grief for what I'd lost and my anxiety about what was to come, and she too was strangely subdued now that we were almost alone together. It was, in truth, the first time we had been so long in each other's company, and neither of us quite knew how to play our respective roles of mistress and maid. The two riders ahead chatted amicably to each other, as did the pair behind, but we trudged in silence right through the day and into the freezing night until we reached an inn close to the harbour, where a room had been prepared for me.

I was stiff and sore as Alise helped me prepare for bed, and not further cheered by Alise telling me the innkeeper's wife had told her of a turn for the worse in the weather during the night. The sea was likely to be choppy tomorrow and there was even speculation about an early fall of snow.

"I have never been on a boat before, milady," Alise said, her eyes wide.

"Don't worry, sailing is good fun," I said, drawing on my recollections of the times Rufus, my sisters and I had crossed the narrow strait, on balmy summer days, to visit my mother's parents in mainland Sweden. Then, despite my grief and fears, I slept well until Alise roused me the next morning, saying we had to leave early to catch the tide.

"Whatever that means," she added, puzzled.

At the harbour, the four servants who had accompanied us so far, handed over our meager luggage to the captain of the tiny boat we were to sail in, and set off back to what I still thought of as my home. I hung round Maise's neck and stroked her muzzle and she nuzzled into me as if she knew she would never see me again. Then I handed her over to the servants and watched with an aching heart as they trotted briskly back up the track, whistling and laughing now that their duties had been fulfilled, and they could get back to their cosy homes and cheerful families.

The captain helped us onto the boat and settled us on fur rugs in the stern "Away from the spray of the big waves, milady." He urged us to wrap more rugs around us as it was likely to be windy when we reached open water. Cold already, I needed no second bidding.

The journey took two days and two nights. It was bitterly cold, the sea was rough and we sailed through hail, biting rain, and a short but heavy fall of snow during the second night.

I have never been so miserable and uncomfortable

in my life, and had no appetite for the food and wine we were offered, but at least I was not sick. Poor Alise though was terribly ill—not even she could make light of her wretched state. But as I tended her and wiped the flecks of vomit from her face, or held a goblet of fresh water to her lips, I was distracted from my own suffering. And I was touched by her obvious gratitude for my feeble efforts to make her comfortable, and by her refusal to complain. She was, I decided, going to be a good companion, and I was glad my mother had chosen her to accompany me.

We must have been a pathetic sight when we reached dry land. I had to support my maid as we got off the boat and walk her back and forth on the harbour front till she felt sufficiently well to continue our journey. Meanwhile, the sailors unloaded our few bags and passed them to the people who had been sent to meet me.

When Alise was strong enough to look after herself I knew it was time for me to acknowledge this welcoming party. I looked up and gasped with shock as I took in the troop of men who were waiting patiently for me. Now, for the first time, I properly registered that I would be moving into a very different role from the one I had played in my father's household. It was like a physical blow. I felt my legs go weak and my heart beat faster with panic and, yes, a certain terrified excitement.

My future husband had sent about a hundred soldiers to meet me. All in smart livery and mounted on tall stallions, so different from the good-natured, but raggedy, bunch that had seen me off from home. My husband. It felt strange to use this word about a man I had yet to meet, and the word jarred uncomfortably in my head, making me feel slightly sick. I turned back to the boat, but the captain had already set sail, the ship's prow riding up and down over the angry waters we'd just crossed. The captain caught my eye and bowed slightly in farewell before turning his attention back to his ropes and sails. Soon this last link with my past life disappeared into the sea mist. I turned slowly back to face my future.

The leader of this grand retinue dismounted as I approached and saluted me, before bowing formally. I dropped a brief curtsey, unsure how a future queen should behave.

"We have fresh horses for you and your maid, when you are ready, Your Ladyship," he said, gravely. He was old and heavily bearded and he spoke with a thick accent, but I could understand him well enough. No doubt my accent sounded strange to him too when I thanked him for attending upon us. Then he smiled and added, in quite a fatherly tone, as if realising my uncertainty as to what was expected of me.

"It is a long way and we will be on the road for two days, but we have good, if simple, accommodation prepared for you, not six leagues hence. May I suggest we start at once? Then you can rest and be fresh for the longer part of the journey tomorrow"

I nodded, glad to fall in with his suggestion, and called to Alise, who had recovered sufficiently to be patting one of the two waiting horses and was smiling and chatting cheerfully to the young man holding them. At a signal from the old man, the younger one brought the horses over and helped me onto an elegant white mare, a much grander beast than my sweet Maise. But she seemed gentle enough, with a mouth sensitive to my commands. Alise was helped onto the other horse and the old retainer fell in beside us as we set off up the road from the harbour.

The weather, though cold, was fine all day, and the snow that had fallen here also during the night, blanketed the land, giving it a magical quality. Sparkling frost twinkled on the branches of the trees in the wintry sunlight and, were it not for my frozen toes and fingers, I felt I could have been passing through fairyland.

We were certainly chilled to the bone and saddle

sore by the time we reached the inn and I would have gladly gone straight to my bed. But the landlord and his servants had prepared a feast in my honour and were clearly proud to have such a distinguished party staying. He appeared anxious to ensure I had nothing but the best his modest establishment could offer, and our chaperone was deferred to on every point regarding the meal and sleeping arrangements.

I was shown to my room to rest briefly and to prepare for the evening meal. I was thankful then that my mother had packed my favourite winter dress in with my luggage. She had told me that, once I was on the mainland, I would not need to wear black in remembrance of my father, but could wear a lighter coloured gown with just a black ribbon to show I was still in mourning. Alise helped me to wash and dress, and then put up my hair like a real lady's.

When she had finished, she departed for the servants' quarters for her meal, whilst I dined with the old man, and a dozen of the more senior officers in the retinue. They talked of the king, their master: his courage, his graciousness, his wisdom and judgement. They talked too, with some indulgent chuckles, of his younger brother who, if I understood them rightly, enjoyed the company of young women rather too much and was a source of worry to his older brother.

I wished that they would talk more of what the king, my future husband, was really like. *Was he tall and handsome? Did he laugh a lot or was he always serious, like my father had been, and bowed down with affairs of state? Did he still mourn for his dead wife? And what had his late wife been like? Had she been a beauty? Was she clever and accomplished? Was she always sweet tempered?* I knew I was spoken of as being tolerably pretty, but my mother had frequently told me off for my sulky appearance in company, and my lack of application to learning anything properly. *Would I be a disappointment in comparison?* But the men did not discuss these points, and I was too timid to steer the conversation that way. Soon I could not help yawning, so Alise was called for and I made my way to bed.

Again, I slept soundly and woke to the drumming of rain on the window shutters. The sky was leaden and the rain had washed much of the snow away, leaving a muddy and desolate landscape. Everything looked dull and damp and grey; it was going to be a miserable day for travelling. I shivered as I looked out of the window, even though the fire in my room had been kept going all night.

Alise came to my room as usual, and helped me to dress.

"Do you know, milady, today is St Lucia's day?"

Of course I knew. The memories from twelve months ago were still raw and painful: my dread of the ceremony, my mother's stern scolding about the need to prepare for marriage and the duties of a wife and lady, and then my brother's awful death, followed by a year of mourning, sickness, uncertainty and further mourning. *How could I forget?* And now I was on a journey from my beloved home to be married and take on the duties of a wife and queen. A queen! It was too much. I was far too timid, far too frail, for such responsibilities.

"No, I hadn't forgotten," I responded, eventually. "But such a lot has happened since last year."

Soon, I could hear the clattering of many hooves in the inn yard. I took a deep breath and tried to gather myself together, but I could not stop the tears that started to run down my face. This time last year I was still a girl, pleading with her mother to be excused from leading the candle-lit procession out of my father's modest abode. Today, I was a woman, about to be escorted by a small army to the much grander establishment of my future husband.

"It's going to be a very different kind of procession

today, from the one last year," I said, between sobs.

Alise, stepping over the boundaries that should be kept between a lady and her maid, took me in her arms and hugged me to her until I stopped crying.

"You will be fine, milady. I'm sure in time you will be a queen known throughout the world. You mark my words."

I shook my head in disbelief. I didn't want to be a queen of any sort, let alone one on the world stage. But I stopped crying, nonetheless, and she wiped my eyes with the edge of her shawl. Together we descended the wooden stairs, and went out into the bone-chilling wind and drizzle to join our new companions.

The old man explained that we had gone inland the day before to avoid the steep cliffs near the harbour and the hilly terrain beyond them. Now we were to turn back towards the sea, and would soon follow the coast path right to our journey's end. I had put my fine dress on again that morning, so as to look at my best when we arrived. But it was made of thinner cloth than the one I'd traveled in so far, and I felt cold from the start of the journey, even though I hugged my cloak close to me, and the innkeeper provided me with an extra blanket.

As we progressed, the old man pointed out to me what, he said, were the finer points of the countryside about us; but all my energies were taken up in fighting the cold and I could simulate little interest. I could see that he too was very cold and I was glad when he eventually stopped talking. We continued for some hours in silence.

Just as dusk was about to fall, and I felt that our journey would never end, we stopped to rest the horses.

"This last half league will take us along the mountainous cliff tops," the old man said, as we walked around on the rapidly re-freezing ground, stamping our feet and rubbing our hands together in a vain attempt to bring life back to them. "But we will not be long now. I will send ahead to report on our progress, so that everything will be ready for you. There will be warm fires and a great feast to celebrate your arrival, you may be sure."

I nodded, too cold to speak, and tried to look as though I appreciated the efforts being made on my behalf. Which indeed I did. But the biting wind, the penetrating rain that had only just eased, and my growing exhaustion and apprehension about what the future held for me, were more pressing on my mind. To keep going without breaking down in tears again was almost beyond me, and I was grateful to have Alise beside me, equally cold but managing a brave smile and a reassuring word, every time I turned to her.

At least it had not started to rain again and the night sky was now clear and starry. Soon, two of the officers I dined with last night jumped back on their horses, doffed their hats at me and set off up the path ahead at a brisk canter, followed by a dozen or so of the other soldiers. The rest of us followed more slowly, but all the horses, sensing they were nearing their destination, and warm stables, had pricked up their ears and were making their way along the steep moonlit path with increasing eagerness.

As soon as the dark outline of a large imposing castle on a rocky outcrop came into sight, the horses broke into a brisk trot, and we clattered into the castle forecourt at such a speed that I was quite out of breath when we arrived. The old man dismounted stiffly, and approached the great door ahead of us where he knocked loudly. Alise also dismounted with a sigh of relief, and she was quickly by my side, murmuring more words of encouragement as she helped me dismount. Then the old man beckoned us to follow him and stood aside as the great door creaked open. I took a deep breath, and stepped forward.

***

"Come brother; do not keep our cousin standing there in

the cold."

I looked up and saw for the first time another man, a lighted candle in his hand, framed in the glow of a great fire at the end of the hall. A big man, regal in his bearing. Older than his brother, who was still stroking my hand, yet not old like my father or the old retainer. His short hair was sable silvered, but his beard was still black and neatly trimmed. His eyes were steel grey and piercing and his mouth firm, though he smiled kindly enough as I approached. His height was remarkable—he was taller than any man I knew—and his shoulders were broad. He seemed to me like a Hercules among men. I could tell at once that this was someone who was used to giving orders, and to them being obeyed. This time, there was no mistaking who this man was: the king, my future husband.

I walked with all the dignity and grace I could muster across the great hall. As I neared the fire, he stepped towards me and reached out his hand. I curtseyed low, my head cast down, and put my lips nervously against his hand.

"Your Majesty," I whispered. He pulled me up gently and looked at me closely. He held the candle so near to my face that I could feel the heat burning my cheeks, whilst the rest of me shivered under his scrutiny.

"The reports do not lie," he said, after a while. "When we are married, Gertrude, you will have as many pretty dresses and jewels as you desire, but I will always remember this meeting and my first sight of you and your sweet natural beauty, even after such a journey. But now, come close to the fire and warm yourself. Welcome to your new home, my beloved. Welcome to Elsinore."

The Tangled Knot

They call me the clown, and clowning is what I do. If I can't make people laugh, I go hungry. But opportunities for laughing, and getting paid for it, are in short supply in my current household, that's why I need to look around. Not that I don't care about my mistress, mind. Or that I don't understand why her current predicament is no joke. Just because I'm a clown, doesn't mean I can't be serious and think. Or that I don't see things that some of my supposed betters are blind to even when it's staring them in the face. That's the life of a clown I suppose. Some of us are better suited to a thinking cap than a hat full of bells. But that's not the life we've been called for. So it's "Hey Ho," and on with the motley, as they say.

Poor Olivia. A countess and a beauty. But she grew up lacking the tender, loving guidance of a mother, and then her father upped and died, too. All she had left in her immediate family was her brother. Her dear, darling brother, her prop and refuge against the world and the responsibilities of state and status, and a fine figure of a man as well. But now he's gone and died.

So Olivia is on her own to run a grand household. Rich, beautiful, clever - and quite unprepared and untrained for her new role in life. She's shy too, though hides it well under a haughty air. But regardless of her seeming composure in public, she simply isn't ready to be a grown-up lady: Too many decisions to make on her own about running the estate and finding a husband. I can see why she wants to hide away

In a properly organised society she shouldn't have to. Make all these decisions on her own, I mean. The estate had been run by her father and handed down to her brother in the normal way—it's no kind of job for a young lady. And as for a suitable suitor—finding one should have been her parents' job, but her father, without a wife of his own to prompt him, had rather let things slip. And then he dropped dead suddenly, and her brother hadn't got around to it before he too passed away. No other brothers, and no sister. At least with a sister she'd have one of her own kind to share her troubles with. A lady's maid is all very well, and in Maria she's got one of the best; so quick witted she'd have made a good clown if she'd been a man. But a lady's maid is there to do as you command, not guide you, tease you, and occasionally scold you. And then make you laugh at yourself. Mind, not even a fully paid up clown manages that all the time, believe me.

Still, I suppose the estate can run itself in the short term, and my mistress has an honest and capable steward in Malvolio to deal with day to day matters. Though, dear God, that man's a bore. My blood turns to snails at the sight of him. Her uncle has moved in to provide some sort of family support too, though the less said about that the better. He seems more intent on drinking her cellar dry, and getting to know Maria rather too well for a household that is supposed to be in mourning. But he's a counter irritant to my lady's grief, I suppose, so she lets him stay. At least he's good company for rest of us (apart from the up-himself steward). And even when he really annoys my mistress— well, being annoyed is better than weeping and moping all day, in my book.

Of course, as soon as word got out she was on her own, potential suitors for her hand (and land) have been two a penny, including her uncle's awful friend, Sir Andrew something-or-other. The most suitable, and the most persistent, is the Duke Orsino, who lives a short gallop away. A good man, a vigorous, manly man, who knows what's what in the world. But Olivia says she can't contemplate marriage to anyone. She's declared she is in extended mourning for her brother during which time she will not consider any proposal. This is quite understandable—buy herself a bit a freedom to mourn, and grow into being a lady and head of this—not inconsiderable—household.

Quite understandable, as I said. *But seven years?* This is a tad excessive by anyone's standards. My guess is there's something more to it than pure grief. Seven years will put her well and truly on the shelf with all the other crusty and dusty old spinsters. *Is that what she wants?* I wonder.

My theory, and bear in mind it's just a clown's theory, is that when her mother died, a little bit of her died too. Then more went when her father died. And, finally, she froze inside completely when her brother died. So she hasn't fully developed. She's a little girl still, in a grown woman's body. Moreover, if you look at it from her point of view; all the people she's loved as a child have brought her nothing but grief and sadness. And then there was no-one left around her to teach her how to love as an adult. Now I suppose she's afraid that if she falls in love with someone, they will just go and die on her too.

I reckon she'll get through it. She's young, she's tough. Yes, she's had a few hard knocks, but she's a survivor. Mind you, I can't see conventional courtship unlocking her capacity to love. It's going to take a catalyst, something—or someone—very special. Maybe a woman's touch... a sister, a girlfriend, a... what's that French word? *Confidante?* Something like that. Someone she can share her feelings with and practice her expressions of love and tenderness on without any negative comeback. She's too proud to admit it, but going the whole hog, and accepting a man's love, and all that that means, if you get my drift, is just too much for her at this stage. So, with no sister to confide in, she needs a girlfriend to tease her out of her mournfulness, or failing that, a eunuch. Though when can you get hold of one of those when you need one? But these are just my theories—and I'm only a clown, like I said.

With so few calls on my time with the Countess Olivia, I've been spending time at the Duke Orsino's place. He professes to be lovelorn for my mistress, but that doesn't stop him from hunting and dining, and paying well for my services. There is still a call for jesting and clowns at his place. He's also taken on a new attendant. Difficult to place what exactly he is; slight build, well spoken, well-mannered and obviously brought up in a gentleman's household. He just appeared out of nowhere and applied to be taken on at the court. Hardly been there five minutes and he's Orsino's most trusted retainer.

But this gentleman is very young, with not a whisker on his chin, and he hasn't entered his full manhood either from the look of him, or the pitch of his voice. Oh, he can swagger about all right if you see him in the street, but it's as if it is an act, like a school pupil acting the man on stage. I've been watching him and, when he thinks no one's looking, like when he and the others are hanging around, waiting for the duke of an evening after a good supper, he droops almost like a woman. And his eyes follow his master round the room like an adoring spaniel. Or lover. He said his name is Cesario, but sometimes, when he's not on his guard, you have to call him two or three times before he responds. And then he blushes, and looks all shifty and discomfited.

Oh yes, there's definitely something odd about that lad, if you ask me. But it's the duke what employs him, not me. And Orsino has trusted him with all his affairs of the heart, so he's off to see my mistress to put the case for the duke. Good luck to him with that—he's got more chance of wooing her himself!

***

And, well, blow me down, knock me over with a feather, strike me with your tickling stick, whatever—with a "hey nonny no," my lady has fallen for the young whippersnapper big time. *Is this the safe eunuch I was after?* Although, and keep this to yourself, I get more the feeling this is the girlie crush I thought my lady needed. No, I'm not convinced that lad is not a lass—not when you see him standing sideways—the contours are in all the wrong places, know what I mean? But, if that's the case, his/her secret's safe with me. There'll be good reason for the disguise I'm sure. And seeing as this young Cesario has managed to cheer up both my mistress and the duke, they'll be wanting to entertain more. Which means there's going to be more work around for a clown. So whatever he/she is up to, it suits me, too. Maybe I can have a laugh or two as well at his expense whilst I'm at it—then we really are all winners. There's not much fun in being a clown. You have to find your own entertainment where you can. A little teasing of the sweet young Cesario isn't going to go amiss by my reckoning.

***

Whee... but things are happening fast round here. My mistress makes no bones about enjoying the company of Cesario, which hasn't upset the duke so far, but has sure made the dim-witted Sir Andrew what-you-ma-call-it jealous. Culminates in a duel of sorts between the pair of them though, in reality, both are too scared to keep their swords up, *pun intended*. But when Sir Andrew tries again a while later, the young man turns and gives him one about the head, and Sir Toby, too. No problem keeping his sword up that time! Must admit, this caused me to doubt for a while my theories about the him/she Cesario.

But just as you think it can't get any more confusing, Olivia turns up and declares her love for Cesario in front of the duke, who says he's going to kill Cesario, who then says he'd rather be killed by the duke than anything else, even (or especially) when Olivia says the pair of them are already married.

Well, I nearly dropped my tickling stick at that. But there is more to come! Suddenly, there are two Cesarios. No doubt about the gender of the new incarnation as he swoops in and kisses Olivia. Turns out the little Cesario we have known for three months really is a woman after all. *What did I say?* And this new apparition is her real flesh and blood twin brother. Both thought the other had been drowned in a shipwreck. Beats me why this meant the young lady had to dress up in boys' clothes and carry on as if she really was her brother in order to get along, but our betters can be pretty weird in their thinking sometimes.

Anyway, seems Olivia married the brother, not the girl, this morning. So that's okay, even if, as the brother says, she would have happily been contracted to a maid the day before. Turns out the duke was falling for his young gentleman too. His/her adoration of him must have been hard to miss, so he's now turned his romantic intentions on the sister. And, if you ask me, he's got a darn sight better chance there than he ever had with my mistress.

So there we have it. If Olivia has married the brother, and Orsino marries the sister, as is definitely on the cards, Olivia will get the sister I've said all along that she needed. And unwittingly, this young Cesario, or Viola, as we must call her now, has been the catalyst to bring Olivia out of her unhealthy mourning habit.

Well, didn't I just say at the outset that a girlfriend-cum-eunuch for a mate was all that was needed? Not that anyone will thank me for such insights. *After all, what do I know?* I'm just a clown.

Toodle-oo!

Our Mad Sister

It's crazy, I know, but it can't be denied that a single woman, of a certain age, is nigh-on invisible. Once I, Cassandra, was the talk of Troy for my fine bone structure, my flawless skin, and my tall, graceful figure. I was clever too, but it was my beauty everyone talked about. I was so beautiful in fact that the god Apollo singled me out to be his lover. I was tempted, of course, who wouldn't be? He too was beautiful with rippling muscles and golden skin. Along with all this he was powerful, both physically and through his god-like status. And so very persuasive; his words would flow like honey and his kisses could have melted a stone.

However I had been blessed, or maybe it was cursed, from a young age with common sense and wisdom. I may have been King Priam's daughter, and sister to the mighty Hector and the flighty Paris, but I could sense that for Apollo I would just be a passing dalliance. I was flattered by his attention, my dreams were full of him, I longed to swoon into his toned, muscular arms, and let him sweep me away with his passionate embraces. My knees went weak and my heart trembled whenever he was near.

But, always, something held me back. I could foresee that for him I was just a novelty, a human plaything he could seduce, before moving on to other paramours. Yes, for him it would be a temporary fancy, before he carried on with his restless pursuit of true love. After which, I would be left as a pregnant pause, burdened with a constant reminder of the shame I had brought onto the royal household. So I held back, resisting his most pressing advances and, eventually, he grew bored with me and left Troy. My common sense, that he had once found so seductive, had started to irk him. Although he knew in his heart that what I said was true, it didn't stop him feeling angry and resentful. As he left, he settled a final curse on me.

"I leave you Cassandra, a frustrated and disappointed god. Your virtue has defeated me. Long may you continue to be sensible," he said. "And long may you be able to foretell the consequences of your, and your compatriot's actions. But you have defied the wishes of a god and, as a mere mortal, you must bear the consequences. I have decreed that no matter what wise words you have to say, no matter what dire events you will foresee—and you will foresee some terrible things - no one will ever believe you. Mark my words: to them you will just be a crazed and embittered old maid, raving at the moon. This is my curse on you, your family and fellow countrymen, for your temerity in refusing a god."

With that he was gone, leaving me bereft, and questioning the wisdom of clinging so tenaciously to my virgin state. *Maybe the passing love of a god would not have been so shameful after all?* The palace was large, and I had my own quarters. True, my parents were getting on a bit and set in their ways, and with old-fashioned notions about courtly behaviour. But they weren't unkind, and times change. Certainly, years later, when Paris snatched the beautiful wife of Menelaus, the Greek, my father was very angry with him, but not so angry that he ordered him to send her back. Instead, he was willing for her to live in the palace, and to let Troy go to war to keep her here. A war I knew was bound to end in our defeat. But no one was listening to me by then.

Oh, the irony! Helen, little more than a pretty tart, arrived in our country, and we were prepared to lose some of our bravest soldiers on her behalf. But then, fathers down the ages have had different standards for their daughters than their sons. Paris carrying on with another man's wife, was easier for him to tolerate now, than his unmarried daughter having a baby with a god. Never mind that it would have been the child of the God of Love, a genuine lovechild, in fact. Back then he had not wanted his clever and beautiful daughter having an illegitimate child, and there was no point trying to make him change his mind. Later, when he might have been more understanding, my chance of motherhood had gone.

So I witnessed my brothers' lives moving on whilst mine atrophied. Hector married the virtuous, but mind bogglingly boring, Andromache; Paris hooked up with his vacuous mistress; and even little Troilus grew old enough to want a woman of his own. Yes, from the shadows, I saw it all. Like Paris, Troilus had an eye for a pretty girl, and his choice, Cressida, was nothing if not pretty. But she was more a Helen than an Andromache. I knew the kind; beautiful, sexy, generous with her favours, and pragmatic in where she bestowed them. I could see she'd dump my brother without a moment's hesitation if she had to; if that's what it took to save her own skin. Then she would bestow her affection on the next man who could provide for her best in the short, if not the long, term. Women like her do not think far ahead, only where the next safe pair of arms are. And they don't ask too many questions about who these are attached to.

Yes, I knew that Cressida would abandon Troilus, and Troy, within days of them supposedly consummating their love, and that she would join her traitor father in the Greek camp outside the walls of Troy. I saw, too, that she would adapt quickly to being a Grecian's mistress. I envisioned just how it would turn out, and I was not wrong! To give her some credit, maybe she, too, had sensed that Troy would soon be overrun.

I could have told my brother all this as I watched him from my balcony, making his way stealthily to Cressida's bed under the cover of a starless night sky. I chose to remain silent. He was young and he'd soon get over any break up, I reasoned. Anyway, what was the point in running out to stop him? He simply wouldn't have believed me, and would probably have denied what he was up to. And then what was I to do? I was just his mad sister, after all.

That's what my brothers called me. "Our mad sister," they used to say to visitors to the palace if I passed them chatting in the corridors. They rarely bothered to introduce me, or to address me by name. I had become old, too old anyway, to be a suitable bargaining chip in a marriage arrangement with neighbouring countries, and too 'odd,' with my true, but ultimately gloomy prophesies, to be welcome in their private quarters as a visitor in my own right. I noticed, but felt powerless to change the fact that, as I grew older and odder, I became less and less important to anyone. Even my parents sometimes forgot who I was.

I was the crazy one, always foretelling doom, pouring cold water on people's plans, and muttering that things would turn out badly for them. Who wants someone like that sitting opposite you over breakfast? Of course I was not always left out, but I was like the poor relation you had to invite to some parties, but you hoped would not cause embarrassment and upset the other visitors. Usually, I was put in a far corner, or at the end of the banqueting table, and admonished to keep quiet and not to talk to any visiting dignitaries. And if I did make one of my, to them, tactless and doom filled predictions, they would cover the ensuing embarrassed silence with a laugh, a roll of the eyes and, maybe, a finger briefly twirled at the temple. Then they would encourage the guests to talk about something else. Later, when things turned out like I had said they would, which they always did, they denied I'd said anything, or blamed me for it, as if any bad event was my fault. Sometimes they did both. And they called me the crazy one!

It wasn't long after Apollo abandoned me that my

beauty started to fade, and people no longer turned admiring glances on me as I walked around the city. Soon they hardly noticed me at all and I, sometimes, had to step off the pavement to let a group of young men through. They never acknowledged this. Why should they? They hadn't noticed me in the first place.

I started to neglect myself; I let my hair grow long and left it to hang loose and uncombed around my neck. Sometimes I even left it weeks before I washed it. The same went with my clothes. Why worry myself about being fashionable and wear things that were uncomfortably tight or long, if no one was going to notice? Instead, I wore my old working smocks for months on end. Soon, I found that people noticed me all right then. Not in a good way. They would look in horror at my eccentric appearance and, fearful perhaps that I was none too sweet smelling, and may want to waylay them and engage them in outlandish talk, they would step into the road to avoid me. At least I got the pavement to myself then. Sometimes I would emit a few cackles, as I drew near to them, and cackle louder whilst they stepped further out into the road to avoid me. Often as not I would shout out too.

"Cry, Trojans, Cry!" was one of my favourites. As well as, "Lend me your ears, and I will fill them with prophetic tears!" This would get them looking anywhere but at me, and scurrying away as fast as they could go. I was not mad, I told myself, because I knew exactly what I was doing and the effect my behaviour had on others. But maybe only a crazy woman would *want* to behave like that. Now there's a thought!

Crazy women didn't spend most of their time in the library though. And this, increasingly was where anyone would have found me, if they had cared to look. I would read almost anything, but history was my main interest. Sometimes this made depressing reading, as the only thing our ancestors seemed to learn from history was that no one ever seemed to learn from history. And, yet, there was so much knowledge there that we could build on including how to govern, how to wage war, how to prevent war, how to live in peace with neighbouring states. Fascinating stuff. I tried, at first, to tell my father and brothers what I was reading about, and how it could help them to govern well, and how they could avoid unwise actions if they did a bit of forward planning. Paris's stupid elopement with the Greek whore, when he was supposed to be on a diplomatic mission, was a case in point.

It was pointless. Priam simply ruffled my hair, and suggested I had a bath and visit my mother more often. And Hector, well Hector, would listen politely, but completely ignore my forebodings. Soon I learnt not to waste my time, and I switched my attention to philosophy, and then to mythology. I realised that this was only a small step away from studying magic and witchcraft, and anyone finding me reading those kind of books would really think I was a mad crone. But I knew I was quite safe. Nobody was likely to want my company enough to come looking for me. I might as well keep my thoughts to myself, and wait in the library for the Greeks to break into the city, as hang about anywhere else. We were all doomed, just like the history books I'd given up reading had foretold.

The siege of Troy seemed to go on forever, we got quite used to peering out over the city walls at the Greeks camped all round. Neither side seemed keen to force the issue and, in my opinion, the Greeks were a pretty disorganised bunch with their chief fighter, Achilles I think they called him, never coming out of his tent. They seemed reluctant to initiate anything without him, so in Troy, after some initial, rather frenetic activity, and the soldiers polishing their armour and sharpening their swords and marching up and down the main street a lot, we got used to the situation. Life ostensibly carried on as normal.

I knew it couldn't last, and I relinquished my

resolution to stay silent to urge my father and brothers to send Helen back. If not, I told them, Troy would burn. But what weight is given to the prophesies of a mad woman, when men sense the opportunity for personal valour, and heroic deeds, to give them a stake in history? I might as well have been whistling in the wind, especially as the uneasy peace still held.

Then came the day when the Greeks finally sent out a challenge. And Hector, earnest, honest and valiant to a fault, took it up. It was all very civilised at first, with him and Troilus visiting the Greek camp to set out the terms, and where dear little Troilus saw his precious Cressida in the arms of another man. Good job he didn't really love her, only thought he did. But he would have been spared even that amount of suffering if he'd taken me into his confidence.

Hector's wife, of course, tried to stop him taking up the challenge, but she was always fearful for his safety, and her words had never held him back before. This was different though, even she could sense it and, desperate, she begged me to help her stop him.

Me? When had anyone listened to me? Of course I knew what would happen when he took up this challenge. He would be killed, his body defiled, and Troy would soon fall to the Greeks. We were coming into the end game. Of course I knew, too, that I would waste my breath trying to say all this to Hector and the others. But poor, sweet, Andromache, was so loyal and loving, I was moved to help her.

I did my best, and even got our father, the mighty Priam on side. But Hector's blood was up and he would not listen, even to him. I shrieked, I wailed, I tore my hair, I rent my garments. All to no avail.

"Oh Hector, Hector's dead." I bellowed, trying to get the ordinary townsfolk to support me in stopping him from leaving the city. But he and Troilus were determined to be heroes, and just saw me as an embarrassment, again, and tried to shoo me away. It was no surprise to me that I had failed to persuade them that, in reality, they were deceiving not just themselves, but also Troy, if they believed Hector could win this challenge. My only consolation was that I had tried my best.

Of course, it worked out exactly as I had foretold. Hector was killed and his body was dragged round behind a Greek chariot for all to see his ultimate degradation. And, as Troy fell and the Greeks swarmed in, the usual murder, rape and pillage ensued. Then my own fate as a captured concubine was sealed. Not pretty. Not pleasant. Definitely a humiliating way for a princess and a scholar to end her days. But, as I think I might have said before, utterly predictable.

Chains of Magic

Senator Brabantio felt he should send his daughter to her private chambers when he realized that Othello, a man of colour, would be among his important guests that night. He wasn't sure what worried him most. Was it only Africans he needed to worry about, or Asians too, or maybe Muslims of any colour, or all of them? All his instincts and upbringing told him he must protect his daughter. Aside from any germs they might carry, or outbreaks of unprovoked violence, there was their attitude to young girls and women. And, oh yes, their gross clasps, their foul charms, their drugs....

His dear wife would have known how to tell the difference between the civilized guests and the drug dealers or rapacious ones, but she had died years ago, leaving him to bring up their only daughter and find her a suitable husband on his own. He was sure his wife would never have regarded a man of colour as a suitable potential husband, but would she have permitted a certain amount of social contact? He puckered his lips anxiously and wished for the millionth time that she were still here to tell him what to do.

Brabantio loved his daughter dearly. He had watched proudly, if timidly, as she grew from a sweet and docile little girl, into an attractive, if sometimes argumentative, adolescent. Now she had blossomed into a beautiful and charming young woman who sat next to him at table as the lady of the house on those occasions when he was required to entertain visiting dignitaries. She was proving to be a great success in this role too. She was excellent at organising the meals and servants so that it all ran smoothly, modest and discrete with all the gentlemen guests, caring and considerate for their wives, knowing just when it was time to leave the men to their port and affairs of state. Her presence at these functions had taken a great weight from his shoulders and he couldn't imagine now how he would manage without her if she ever did marry and leave him to run someone else's household.

But he had other things to worry about tonight. This Othello, the celebrated Moor of Venice, the brave general, was due to visit. True, he was not a young man. Almost the same age as Brabantio himself. And he was definitely a very important person. But he was black. Very black. A Muslim, too, by all accounts. *Should he run the risk? Would he not still, despite his age and rank, exude some kind of dusky charm that would intoxicate a young woman? Even one as shyly modest and level-headed as Desdemona?* He wrung his hands. No, he couldn't take the risk.

Then what? How would he get through the evening on his own? Wouldn't all his usual guests notice her absence and find it strange? How would he explain why she wasn't there? Would they laugh and think him old-fashioned if he gave his reasons? What sort of embarrassment to the state would that cause, if the great Othello himself found out?

But what if she did attend? Wouldn't those same guests accuse him of being careless with her reputation in letting her sit at table with such an exotic? Would she be tainted by such contact? Would that make her less easy to marry to someone suitable? If only that young man who was so intent on wooing her at the moment wasn't such a drunken fop. If only Desdemona had shown some sign she was remotely interested in his attention. Why, then he could have agreed the match months ago and wouldn't have all this worry. True, he had told this... what was his name? Roderigo? ... himself that he didn't want him as a son-in-law. Despite the young man's rank and background, he was not the upright and intelligent man he had envisaged as suitable for his daughter. But he wouldn't be in this quandary if Desdemona was now betrothed to him, or someone like him. Perhaps he should have tried harder to encourage the courtship.

Oh, if only his dear wife were here... or if only the lusty moor, *for he was sure he must be that, despite his age*, could be sent off quickly on some new campaign so wouldn't have time to dine with him tonight. He wrung his hands again and groaned.

"What is it, Father?" Desdemona had entered without him hearing. She kissed him gently on the cheek. "Still worrying about affairs of state? I'm sorry I can't help you there, but I have sorted the seating plan for dinner tonight." Brabantio jumped as if shot. "Oh, my dear daughter, I'm not sure you should be there at all. What would your dear mother...."

"I'm sure Mother would have been at your side, as I will be," Desdemona replied, firmly. "Why, do you think the noble Othello is going to try and cast a spell on me over the soup?" She laughed merrily, and Brabantio joined in weakly.

"It's true, I'm dying to meet him, to hear from him about his adventures. Has he really met people who carry their heads beneath their shoulders? And he is so brave by all accounts."

"He is a noble man, as good as any," Brabantio agreed, hesitantly. "But, daughter, he is black. Such men aren't like the rest of us; they cast spells on young women... minerals... medicines...."

"Which is why I have placed him next to me, in case any of our female guests are nervous, or he lacks those soft parts of conversation they are used to."

"Oh, daughter!" Brabantio looked aghast, and Desdemona patted him affectionately.

"Dear father, don't be so old-fashioned! I'm a

grown woman. And, apart from anything else, he is so old! No, you just leave the arrangements for the evening to me. I'll see that he is properly entertained according to his rank and fame. I'll get cook to serve your favorite pudding— grilled figs with butter and honey and a sprinkle of cinnamon, just how you like them. Now, I'm sure you have plenty of other things to do today. You just go and sort your state papers out for the next senate meeting. And don't worry!"

She ushered him gently toward his office, pecking him on the cheek again before dropping a brief curtsey and departing towards the kitchen to have a word with the housekeeper and head cook.

Brabantio hesitated before entering his office. He had felt helpless to argue. Desdemona could be very persuasive when she wanted to be and, in truth, he really loved sticky fig pudding. He would have been lost without her to sort the dinner arrangements. *But was it what his wife would have agreed to? Would she herself have sat down with a black man, however noble? And would she have allowed her unmarried daughter to sit next to one?* He doubted it. *Oh dear, what troubles had he unleashed upon himself?* He was sure no good was going to come of such a break from custom. His daughter would be doomed to spinsterhood, and he would be the laughing stock of Venice.

Sighing, and wringing his hands even more desperately than before, he finally entered his office and spent the rest of the day wrestling with his nervous indigestion, blinking queasily at his papers, deferring any important decision till he felt better, and praying to God and any saint who might be listening, that the evening would pass without incident. If only his dear wife was still around to tell him what to do....

***

Desdemona meanwhile spent a productive afternoon discussing menus with the cook, supervising the preparation of the dining hall, and arranging table decorations with her lady in waiting. She was excited. Most of the dinners her father held were dull affairs with elderly men and their elderly wives in predominance. The talk was always about politics and commerce, in neither of which she had any interest. Sometimes, she struggled to stay awake and the talk, when the ladies withdrew and wanted to discuss the servant problem or their ailments, was scarcely more enlivening. But tonight there would be the great Othello himself and other serving soldiers of rank—the conversation was bound to be more thrilling both during, and after, the meal.

She wouldn't dare to say anything herself of course. She was still shy and blushed profusely when directly addressed, which made her even more tongue-tied. There was so much she would like to ask the general, and she hoped her father and his friends would be as curious as she was to know more of his adventures and the places he had visited. Maybe she could prompt her father before the meal. Or would he think her too interested, too immodest even, and all his worries about her being there at all would resurface? No, perhaps she had better leave it to fate. After all, if Othello was to be in Venice for any length of time, he would have to be invited again. It might take time for her curiosity to be satisfied, but she was patient, and a good listener.

She was a good organiser, too. She was quite confident in her ability to ensure all the guests were well looked after. The cook had told her the general probably wouldn't eat pork or shellfish so she had opted for roast swan, lamb, and venison with a wide range of baked, boiled and steamed vegetables. All washed down with the best wine her father's cellar could offer. Plenty of choice would ensure there would be something to suit everyone's taste. The main courses would be followed by the sponge and sorbet gateau, decorated in true Venetian style, the cook had promised for dessert. To finish, there would be plenty of fruit: dates from North Africa, grapes and oranges from Spain, even a few apples from England, though they were now a little soft following their long journey. And, of course, the grilled figs.

She heard her stomach rumble as she thought of the feast to come. She had been too busy to stop for lunch, and now she needed to go and bathe and dress for the evening. There would be no harm, surely, in her wearing her new gown, and her mother's lovely pearls that her father had given her when she came of age? She was not particularly vain and rarely took long over her toilet, even for important functions, but she knew the pearls showed off her long, delicate, white neck to advantage, and the rich azure brocade of her dress matched exactly her blue eyes. She had a premonition that it was going to be a night to remember, and she wanted to dress the part.

***

Although she had confidently assured her father that it was best to place Othello next to her so as not to offend or upset any of the other female guests, Desdemona found herself even shyer than usual at table, and far too nervous to look directly at their special guest. But she soon realized that, although he had spoken to her civilly on arrival and she had murmured a few words in response, there was no need for her to speak at all. The questions from the men were all about Othello's exploits and he was happy to elaborate on them.

She listened, gripped, as he told them of his battles, sieges, and accidents. His capture and escape from slavery, his travels and his meetings with cannibals—and yes, he really had been to the land where there were men whose heads grew beneath their shoulders. Desdemona was so engrossed she could hardly breathe. She often forgot to signal to the servants to clear the plates for the next course and had to be prompted by the chief steward. Her father had to remind her twice that it was time for her to retire with the other ladies.

Only as she rose to leave the dining hall did she pluck up enough courage to look directly at Othello and, with a small sigh, express her sorrow for the sufferings he had endured and admiration for the courage he had shown in combating them. He had risen too, bowing to her as she left the table and taking her hand to kiss. She did not resist and as she caught his eye, he smiled at her with such attentiveness that her heart raced and she felt the blood rushing to her cheeks. Not just a man of courage, she knew instinctively he must also have a constant, loving, and noble nature. No one could look at a woman like that if they did not. He was just the kind of brave but tender man she had dreamt of for a husband.

She blushed more deeply than she had ever done before, confused, and embarrassed by this unbidden train of thought. Quickly, she withdrew her hand from his and almost ran out of the room without looking back. The other ladies hurried after her.

***

The men seemed to take forever over their port and conversation dragged amongst the ladies. They, too, had all seemed fascinated at table by Othello's tales, but were too refined to be the first to mention him or them. Yet other topics seemed pallid by comparison. Desdemona tried to show an interest in her companions' health and family doings, but her mind was elsewhere and she was relieved when, finally, her father called to say the men were ready to go. She rallied a little then to bid her guests farewell and wish them safe journeys home, but retreated to her chamber as soon as the last one had departed. Normally, she and her father would chat a little together each night before retiring but it was late and, she reasoned, he would be tired—his health was not good and the dinner would have been a strain for him.

Desdemona herself was not tired. She was glad her lady in waiting had been in already to turn down the covers and light the small bedside lamp. She changed quickly into her nightdress and climbed into bed. She had no desire to read, but instead closed her eyes and thought back excitedly over the conversation at dinner. Othello had lived a life so different from her own and her father's. Neither of them had been beyond the city walls in her lifetime as Brabantio had been reluctant to travel on business and he was now far too old to be called up for combat.

The stories Othello told of strange lands and extraordinary incidents had been a feast in themselves, but she was hungry for more. Such dangers had he faced and lived to tell the tale! Her father must invite him again—and again. She was sure he would, but if he were reluctant, she would use all her subtle powers to persuade him. Of course, she realized, to seem too interested would only worry Brabantio, so she would have to be careful.

Othello's stories had cast a spell on her but she was going to learn from this and use her own charms on her father to ensure the noble general was invited again. She would remind her father that the moor was destined to be of continuing service to the state so he, Brabantio, leading senator, was obliged to entertain him generously. She could organise bigger and better meals on his behalf, and could hide her curiosity behind her customary maidenly modesty whilst finding out more about the man she loved.

She gasped and sat up straight in bed. Love! What was she thinking! Othello, The Moor of Venice, could have no thought of marrying her, a mere slip of a girl - and white as a lily, too. Besides, she had been too shy to speak to him that evening, and would never be allowed to be alone in his company nor did she know anyone she could confide in, or use as a go-between.

How could he get to know of her passion without her courting criticism for forward behavior? Maybe he would know anyway, without her needing to say anything, and would ask one of the young officers who accompanied him to dinner to intercede? Her father would see nothing amiss there. After all, he was not averse to her finding a husband. She thought of all the other young men, potential noble matches, that he had suggested and whom she had dismissed as too boring.

As for her latest suitor... her nose wrinkled in disgust. She was glad her father did not like him either, and had told him his daughter was not for him. But it was someone of his ilk, if somewhat more sensible, that her father would definitely want her to settle down with eventually. Someone of rank and standing in the city; steady, industrious, ambitious, careful. He would happily marry her to such a man, and stand by proudly as she set up her own household and produced several grandchildren for him over the years. It was a life she had envisioned for herself with equanimity, if not actual enthusiasm. Until now. Now she would rather die than end up with such a fate. It was the moor or a convent for her. No other man would do.

Dare she forsake her friends and father? Surely they would not approve of such a match. Dear father, the shock would kill him! Her confidence failed for a moment, she really loved her father and did not want to hurt him, but he would never consent to such a son in law, and it would be dangerous to her cause to ask him to consider it. However, his anxieties and hesitancy about all the little things in life would drive her mad if she had to live at home much longer. They were already driving her crazy, she had to admit. She yearned to be at the side of a man of action, a man of passion—her lusty moor! She stifled a giggle. *What was she thinking of?*

She would have to use her own chains of magic to draw him to her until he, and he alone, could see her love for him, and reciprocate. They would have to elope of course, and then cast their fate upon the mercy of the senate. But it would be worth it. She would marry the moor, or die in the attempt.

By now she was quite tired, and the excitement of the early evening was catching up with her. Yawning, she drew her white, silk sheets up around her chin with one hand and smoothed them down over her breasts and thighs with the other. Just like a wedding dress, she thought dreamily as she looked down on her white-draped, shapely body. Soon, she thought, I will be fast asleep. *Dear God, will it be a sin if I dream of such a secret courtship, of strange lands, and of this man who now seemed to her to be more fair than black?*

Othello would be coming to the house again very soon, she was sure of it; the next day even. Tomorrow! Yes, tomorrow was when she would start her campaign to charm him into loving her. She would ask cook to prepare something special. Not oysters of course, as Othello would not be able to eat the shellfish, however delicious, but something just as powerful. Asparagus perhaps? Her newly betrothed friend had sworn by them. Asparagus tips steamed until just al dente to retain their potency, then lightly tossed in melted butter and sprinkled with flower pollen.

And if that didn't work she would cast her own spells and win him with magic. She could! She should! She would! He was the breath of life to her. Smiling happily to herself, she reached up and put out the light.

A Virtuous Maid

What in Heaven's name was I thinking of? I must have been mad! Yes he said he was a friar, but a most unlikely one, wandering in and out of prisons and places at will. He's new to Vienna too - at least *I've* never met him before, or heard mention of him, even. Come to think of it, I still don't know his name, or what religious establishment he's linked to. And, yet, I've just agreed to go along with his plan which, he says, will preserve my virtue and save my brother's life without causing death or dishonour for anyone. Dear God, these are unchartered waters for me.

Until today, I knew what I was destined for; I was to be a bride of Christ following a life of piety, prayer, and penitence. And chastity. But just as the nunnery gates were about to close, embracing me in a cloistered life, sordid earthly matters have burst upon me, disrupting all my plans, and dragging me back out into the world again.

Oh, if only I had joined the nuns the day before. The gates would have already clanged shut, my vows of silence would have been whispered to the reverend mother, and I would have been free at last of mundane worries. Instead, I am still in the world, still permitted to talk to men and walk about the city on my own, still expected to concern myself with the lives of family and erstwhile friends who were living and dying beyond the nunnery walls. This loud, messy, carnal world I had yearned to leave, has seemed intent on drawing me back. But I am not to be drawn. I am quite decided on that, whatever the calls made upon me.

It was the friar who approached me, and said he understood my predicament, and perhaps he could help. Oh, he was very kind, and very persuasive, and I had no one else to advise me. I had been praying hard for guidance, but none came. It seemed it was God's will I made my own decision. Maybe it was his last test of my will before my dedication to Christ. Maybe he was too busy. Maybe my problems were too trivial, too mundane.

But was this the right answer? The friar's plan was preposterous: incredible, and scarcely honourable. I would be mad to go along with it. But what were the other options? Could I just walk away, lock myself back in the nunnery, and forget the whole episode? If only God had given me even the smallest indication of His wishes. But there'd been nothing, and the Friar had urged me to be quick in carrying out his plan, no time for second thoughts, a man's life depended on it.

Something still felt wrong, but what am I, apart from an insignificant young woman, not much more than a girl really, a virgin clinging onto my virtue for dear life? Who am I to question the wisdom of a holy man? And yet... Oh, has the whole world gone mad? I will be glad when I can turn my back on it, just as soon as I have carried out the friar's request. But God, I wish you had sent me some sign to let me know that what I'm going to do is your will.

***

My name is Isabella. Some people call me pretty. My parents certainly did when they were alive. But my good looks have never been of interest to me. I have known from an early age that I had a vocation, and I have dedicated my life to fulfilling it. From childhood I knew that as soon as I was old enough I would devote myself to God by becoming a nun. It's been hard to wait so long, but not so hard to resist the temptations of the world. That's how I knew I had a vocation—I positively looked forward to a life of discipline and denial.

My brother Claudio is completely different. Dear Claudio, my closest living relative, is so strong and handsome, so full of life and vigour that even the birds tweet louder when he is around. He certainly doesn't have a vocation, unless you call being the life and soul of any gathering a vocation. How that boy loved... loves... life. And how everyone he meets loves him. I will miss him and his laughs and boisterous affection when I take the veil, but not enough to make me change my mind. Sweet memories of our childhood closeness will keep me strong. And I know he will be happy, when he thinks about it, to know that his sister is happy too, and doing what she wants. Besides, he loves my cousin Juliet and she loves him.

They are to be married—the sooner the better, everyone says, since she is carrying his baby. Indeed the marriage should have taken place before I entered the nunnery, but the duke, who oversees such things, suddenly went away on business, and the wedding had to be postponed. I have prayed he will be back soon, and that it will take place before the baby arrives, so the little one will be legitimate in the eyes of the church. But such matters will shortly be out of my hands.

I joined the Saint Clare nuns as soon as I was old enough. We are supposed to be one of the strictest nunneries, one of the most secluded from the world, with only the very basic concessions to creature comforts. But from day one I loved it—my whole life to be spent without distractions from prayer and contemplation. Indeed I would have welcomed fewer privileges and planned to beg for harsher conditions once I became a full sister. I was hungry and eager to serve God with all my body and soul. I couldn't wait to join the sworn nuns. Indeed, I was talking about this with one of them when a man called at the nunnery gates and, as the only one not yet fully sworn, so still allowed to speak to men, I was sent to deal with him.

What a man! I recognised him as an associate of my brother's, though he didn't recognise me in my wimple. Lucio by name; loud mouthed and saucy by nature. True, he did try to behave in a more seemly fashion than he usually did in front of a young woman because, as he said, by coming to speak to an inmate at St Clare's, he was almost talking to the saint herself. I didn't like his manner none-the-less, and I started to turn away, but he stopped me in my tracks when he said he was looking for a particular novice nun. He needed to talk to her about her unhappy brother Claudio.

Of course that was me, so I had to ask what Claudio was unhappy about. Oh horror! Claudio has been thrown into prison and sentenced to death for getting Juliet pregnant. I know he shouldn't have, and Juliet shouldn't have let him. It's against God's will and the law of the land. But, alas, the offence is all too common. It isn't right, but the duke has tolerated a premature anticipation of conjugal felicity for years, provided the couple do marry in the end.

"But Claudio and Juliet want to get married!" I exclaimed. "Why can't we wait for the duke to return? He'll be only too happy to see them wed."

Lucio shook his head. It seems the duke's deputy, one Angelo, has taken advantage of the duke's absence to crack down hard on law breakers—especially those committing sins of the flesh. And so my brother is to die unless, that is, according to Lucio, I can persuade Angelo to forgive him and let him go. I was happy to agree. Lustful and sinful though he has been, Claudio is still my brother and I could not in my heart feel this to be a capital offence.

The reverend mother frowned, but didn't raise any objections to me going on this errand. In fact, she wished me well, but told me to hurry back once I'd spoken to the deputy, as I was scheduled to take my vows the next day. Maybe she was worried I would be tempted by worldly pleasures once away from the nunnery, but she needn't have worried. I'd never been tempted before, and I was sure of my chosen vocation.

I was sure, too, I could persuade Angelo. After all, I

agreed with him totally about the need to tighten up on the loose morals of the city. And I could concede that sending Claudio to prison was a clear message to others to be more cautious in their relationships outside marriage. But Claudio was not the worst sinner in this respect, not least because he really did want to marry Juliet. And how was she to manage, an unmarried mother, if he was put to death? Should an unborn, innocent, babe be condemned to a life as a social outcast because of the sins of the parents? Surely these arguments, and my own manifest virtue, would persuade the just and upright Angelo that Claudio came from a godly family and, ultimately, his intentions were honourable?

I did my best but, alas, Angelo was not to be persuaded by my entreaties. Not even when he asked me to visit him again the next day. I agreed to return, hoping to change his mind at the second attempt after he had had a night to think about his response. Praying that his stern and unrelenting approach could be tempered by mercy on this occasion.

But I had so misjudged this man. He is bad. Evil! Far, far worse than Claudio, whose zest for life and love for Juliet had led him into sinful ways. It was true, Angelo had changed his mind during the night. But his new proposal was simply wicked. Claudio's life might be saved, he said, if I would sleep with him, Angelo, in exchange.

Surely this could not be God's will? For a man to go with a whore is bad enough, a sin that Angelo has rightly cracked down on. But for him then to desire to violate a virgin, a future bride of Christ, is so unspeakably worse. And what of her child if he made her pregnant?

With Angelo, I felt I was in the presence of the very devil. Oh, he talked of 'love' and 'honour,' but threatened worse for Claudio if I did not comply. So where is the love and honour in that? My brother wouldn't expect such a sacrifice from me. Not even to save his neck. He would understand. My chastity is more important than his mortal life. For him to be executed would be for him to die just the once. For me a nun, albeit still a novice, to sleep with Angelo would be to sentence my soul to perpetual limbo.

***

I had done my best to save my brother's life, and I'd failed. Sadly, I went to the prison to explain this to him, pray with him, and reconcile him to death. That was when I first met the strange friar. I scarcely spoke to him when I arrived, but went straight to meet my brother and gave him the sad news of my doomed intercession on his behalf. Poor Claudio, all his vivacity gone, just the exhausted hope that he might be reprieved. When I told him the conditions Angelo had set for this, that it would be like incest for him to take life from his sister's shame, he agreed at once. My sweet, noble brother could not countenance the thought of me losing my virtue in such a way.

But then he went even paler than he was before, and I could see that the prospect of imminent death just terrified him. He begged me to re-consider for his sake. The coward! That my own brother should expect such a sacrifice from me. Is death so very fearful, when there is the prospect of Heaven in the hereafter? I couldn't bear to be with him any longer and tried to leave quickly. I promised to pray for him, but he kept on pleading with me, and holding me back. Then the friar came in again.

By this time I was desperate to get back to the nunnery and get on with my life of devotion, but the friar took me to one side. I felt perhaps he wanted to calm me down, although I would have thought Claudio was in greater need of his ministrations. Anyway, he did in fact calm me—his voice and manner were so gentle and soothing.

Then he told me a story about another woman that Angelo had been engaged to, whom he had abandoned when she lost her dowry. Despite this she was still pining for him and would, he was sure, be willing to go in my place, whilst pretending to be me, and sleep with Angelo. That way, said the friar, Claudio would be saved, my virginity would be preserved, and Angelo would have to marry the fiancée he'd abandoned, once he was confronted with what he'd done. A mad scheme, I know, but the friar convinced me it would all work, and would be God's will. So I agreed.

But why did I agree? Wasn't I putting another woman in jeopardy? Maybe that was for her to decide, not me. If she thought her future happiness was secure with Angelo, even if ultimately she would be tricking him into marriage, then God be with her. And she had my blessing, too. After all, he was still, in law, her intended husband.

And Claudio would be saved. Only then could I admit to myself how important my brother's life was to me. *Could I really have withdrawn from the world, knowing I had left him to go to his death? Would God really have wanted me to do that?* The friar had been so reassuring. I had faith in him even if he didn't seem much like any other friar I had met. His faith, or maybe it was just him as a person, was magnetic and I felt irresistibly drawn to him. There was something so noble about him that he overcame all my reservations about his proposal. I dread seeing Angelo again, but will do, just the once, to agree the tryst. I'm looking forward to seeing the friar so we can carry out his plan.

Maybe he will want to see me again too, when it's all over. But, of course, he won't be able to. Once this is all sorted I will be straight back to the nunnery to take my vows and disappear from the world. Never more to speak to a man alone. Exactly as I have yearned for all my life.

Only... only I do so want to spend more time with the friar. If I could just know his name and where he came from, and why he has chosen to help me and my brother. He seems so virtuous. Worldly, too, but in a good way. I feel I could spend my life listening to him talk, and following his advice. Forever.

Is this so very shocking? I find myself blushing and trembling as I think of him. My heart is racing so much I fall to my knees. *Is this God's will in action? That I spend the rest of my life with the friar, rather than the nuns? Goodness what on earth am I thinking of?*

Conjuring the Moon

The day started as usual. She loved the tranquility of her own room in the quiet of the early morning. A short time to herself away from the bustle and intrigue of the court, away from the draughty state rooms and the stifling etiquette. And away, too, from her meddling, quarrelsome sisters. But today her peace was shattered when the door burst open and both her sisters entered. They were out of breath as if they had been vying with each other as to who would get to her chamber first.

Cordelia put down the tapestry she was working on and looked up warily. Just one of them visiting was a rarity, as each had given up expecting her to take sides in their daily arguments, and neither appeared to have any other use for her. Both coming together to see her did not bode well.

Goneril banged the door behind them none too gently and Regan followed her usual habit on entering a room of going straight over to the mirror to check her appearance. She tweaked her hair a bit, lifted up her breasts in her bodice and re-arranged her necklaces, turning this way and that in front of the tiny looking-glass in the corner, to ensure she was presenting her ample décolletage to best advantage.

"When you've quite finished, sister," Goneril spoke to her sharply, tapping her fan impatiently on her hand.

"Yes, of course," Regan smiled back at her sister, though there was no warmth in her smile, or her voice, or her eyes, as she turned her face towards Cordelia.

"I don't know why you bother with such a stupid little glass, and in such a dark corner too. No wonder you look such a mess when you come down to dinner." My sister's smile could curdle milk thought Cordelia, not for the first time.

"To what do I owe the pleasure?" she asked, rising from her seat. With difficulty she kept her voice soft and low, but her sisters scared her and she felt she would be more comfortable without them towering over where she sat. Even when she stood though, they still had the advantage. Both took after their mother, a big-boned, statuesque, matron who had died in childbirth when Cordelia was born nearly five years after her sisters. Cordelia wasn't sure who she took after, though her father often said she reminded him of his favourite sister. She had died of pneumonia before she was twenty, not much older than Cordelia was now.

Goneril picked up the tapestry from the low table where Cordelia had placed it, examined it briefly before snorting, and tossing it down so carelessly that it missed the table, and fell onto the floor. Cordelia stooped and picked it up.

"To what do I owe the pleasure?" she repeated, keeping tight hold of the tapestry this time, as if afraid Regan too would want to snatch it from her. They had, after all, managed to break all her dolls between them as she was growing up, and these days still 'accidently' tore her dresses before special events, or mislaid her shawls on cold days.

"Oh do sit down, Cordy." Goneril spoke with her usual shortness, as she pulled up a chair for herself by the little table. There were only two chairs, and Regan was still standing, but Cordelia felt it was prudent to sit. She knew which sister to fear the most: although Goneril had been lucky in marrying a decent, mild - mannered man, his good nature had not, to date, had any noticeable effect on his wife's capacity for calculated bullying and meanness. Regan, the middle one, could rant and rave, and often did, but she was unable to carry through a devious plan unless Goneril was there to direct her.

"Our father is bonkers. Oh don't look at me in that

pained way, Cordy, you know full well he's been doing some very odd things over the last few years, and it's getting worse. He leaves all matters of government now to those stupid old farts Kent and Gloucester whilst he goes off hunting and drinking with his men or gibbering in corners with that fool of a court jester."

"He didn't go to bed at all last night, too drunk I suppose. They found him this morning fast asleep in the stables with nothing on but his crown." Regan tittered as she spoke.

Cordelia looked up at her sister and took a deep breath.

"But you know full well, Regan, my lord the Duke of Cornwall—your husband—put something in his drink last night as he thought it would be amusing to see what happened. I heard Goneril's husband, my lord the Duke of Albany, remonstrating with him. He felt it was wrong to compromise the dignity of the king like that."

"Why, you little bitch, how dare you bring our husbands into it?" Regan went to grab a lock of Cordelia's hair, but Goneril put her hand up to stop her.

"We are digressing sisters," she said, curtly. "We have come to see you, Cordy, as the king, our father, just as Regan's dear husband planned, is now convinced after last night's performance that he no longer has the ability to rule the country. He is set on dividing his kingdom between the three of us and our husbands at once, rather than after his death. Which means you'd best hurry up and choose which of your suitors you are going to have, my girl." She leant forward and tweaked Cordelia's cheek sharply as she spoke. "And neither of them will be in a hurry to pick you if you don't make a bit more effort. Here you are at nearly noon and still no make-up on."

"Any man I marry will want me for the kind of woman I really am, not for my appearance, or my lands," Cordelia said, rising to her feet again, and struggling to contain her growing anger.

"Bollocks!" Goneril retorted. "Any husband you get is going to want you for the land and money you bring with you, you stupid dwarf. And, believe me, if he's going to enjoy begetting heirs by you he'll want you to at least look fuckable, not like some dowdy pigmy." Cordelia went pink with anger and embarrassment at this, and Regan again tittered, repeating to herself over and over. "Fuckable, fuckable."

"Oh do belt up Regan, if you can't contribute anything constructive at least keep your mouth shut."

Regan poked her tongue out at her sister's back, but said nothing more as Goneril turned to Cordelia with a chilly lightheartedness.

"So, come on, kiddo. Smarten yourself up and get yourself down to the great hall in half an hour."

Cordelia sat down again. She knew full well her father's judgement was failing and with that his ability to rule effectively. But, as far as she could see the Earls of Gloucester and Kent, when he was in the country, were still able to steer him towards reasonably sensible decisions most of the time. She had always known that the kingdom was to be divided three ways on his death, but had felt no need to trouble herself with the detail. After all, Lear was still physically strong, he could live for several more years and she saw no reason why he could not reign until his death with the right support. She didn't like, or trust, Regan's husband, but Goneril's husband had offered wise judgement and support to the king on a number of occasions recently. And she too, with the right husband, could support and protect him from the increasing ravages of old age.

What, apart from being humiliated by Cornwall overnight, had made him suddenly move his plans forward? Did Kent and Gloucester know? And if so, did they think it wise? What would Lear do with himself if he divided up his kingdom? Where would he live? Who would care for him? Has anyone given these matters any consideration? She doubted it, and the more questions that came into her mind, the more concerned she became about the hurried way in which this turn of events seemed to have come about.

Whilst she sat and pondered, Goneril was rummaging in her wardrobe and Regan was fiddling around in her make-up box. After a few minutes Goneril turned to face her, holding out one of her dresses.

"Ye Gods, I never realised what a pathetic range of frocks you had. Nothing to show off your assets, pathetically small though they are. And some of these dresses are quite ripped! But this one should do, you can hide the tear under a shawl. Now where are they? Oh, never mind, I'll lend you the one I'm wearing, it's a good colour match. It's in all our interests today to get you married off as soon as poss. So put a move on. Get dressed properly and get yourself down to the great hall sharpish, whilst we go and find our husbands. Regan, what the hell are you doing?"

Regan looked round shiftily. "Oh, just sorting some suitable make-up for Cordy." She held up a block of rouge. "You haven't started this yet. Seeing as you don't like it, I might as well have it." She didn't wait for permission, but placed it in her reticule, and bestowed on her sister another chilly smile as she swept towards the door after her sister. She paused at the threshold.

"Oh, in case you're wondering, two of your suitors, France and Burgundy, have been sent for too. So it's make your mind up time little sis. Ciao!" and she was gone.

Cordelia picked up the shawl Goneril had thrown down as she left and smiled wryly. Over the past few weeks, she had wondered where her new paisley shawl had disappeared to or, more precisely, which sister had taken it. But Goneril was right. It would go quite well with the dress she had picked out for her. And the shawl would indeed cover that new tear across the right shoulder. Such consideration was unusual. Clearly Goneril set a lot of store on Cordelia choosing a husband that day.

But Cordelia was worried. It couldn't simply be the need for the three sisters to be married to trigger this sudden division of the kingdom. *What else was at stake? What more was needed? What was it that her sisters were keeping from her?* She felt sick as she dressed and applied her make–up. As she looked into her mirror she could see that she was unusually pale, even for her. Worry about what was in store had drained the blood from her face. She could have done with a touch of that rouge Regan had just removed from her make-up box. Instead, she pinched her cheeks and bit her lips until some colour returned.

'And what is it that I'm worried about exactly?' she was honest enough to ask herself. 'My father's health and judgement? My chance of a share of the kingdom? My future husband? Wasn't that still for Lear to decide?

She thought of Burgundy; tall, dark, handsome, charming, his English fluent, eloquent even. Her heart beat a little faster as she thought of the many pretty turns of phrase he used when they talked, and how he could almost convince her that she was the most beautiful woman in the world. But her head reminded her that his dukedom was desperately short of money, that his father had instructed him to find a rich bride, that he would not be unaware of the money and land she was due to inherit on her elderly father's death. The chance to get his hands on them sooner rather than later would be irresistible.

Then she thought of France. A gentle and modest man; rather earnest, but interesting and amusing enough when he got over his diffidence. His kingdom was small, and there were recurring problems with minor uprisings in the provinces, but on the whole his position was secure. Albany liked him, she knew, and Cornwall mocked him behind his back for being a boring drinking companion and a tediously upright prig on issues of morality and ethics. Not that Cornwall would understand matters of conscience anyway, so this was hardly condemnation of the young king in Cordelia's eyes.

But what did she really want? Would she prefer the heady excitement of marriage to Burgundy, followed by pain and sadness when he grew bored of her company as, even in her youth and inexperience, she knew would be almost inevitable with a man like that? Or would matrimony be better in France, alongside a steady and sensible young man with whom there was a chance that their existing mutual respect and compatibility could grow into true love? A man she was sure could match her sense of duty, and would care for her aging father in his declining years.

She knew what the right answer was, but she was young enough, and romantic enough, to feel a slight wistfulness at the possibility of missing out on full bloodied, heady, if transient, passion.

She finished combing her hair and turned from the mirror a little fretfully. *Why was she worrying herself about this anyway?* Despite her sister's dig about making up her mind, she knew full well the choice was not hers to make, only that she could refuse if she was really unhappy about a proposal. Lear may have already decided for her, and she was not accustomed to going against her father's wishes. She would just go down now, be told her fate, and accept it graciously and calmly. Her father would have her best interests at heart, as he always had. All the same....

She peered for one last time into the dim mirror. Goneril's right, she sighed, I am a little homespun thing. She patted her cheeks again to revive the colour, but it was too late now to make any major adjustments. She turned away from the mirror, gathered her shawl around her, and stepped out of her room.

***

As she approached the great hall she could hear voices and, turning the corner into the light, she found her two sisters, their husbands and a number of followers already waiting. Goneril turned, and eyed her up and down with a look of contrived dismay.

"Oh dear, that shawl doesn't really go with that dress very well, after all," she said, after a pause. The others also turned. Regan started her usual tittering behind her fan, but the Duke of Albany stepped forward and gave his young sister-in-law a small bow.

"You look absolutely charming," he said, taking her hand and drawing her into the group. Cordelia smiled at him gratefully, and Albany was, as ever, taken by her dignified demeanour. But the Duke of Cornwall merely sniffed.

"Just as well," was all he had to say in response to his brother-in-law's chivalry.

"Why don't we go in?" Cordelia asked no one in particular.

"The king has not yet arrived," Goneril replied. "Which gives me time, dear sisters, to coach you on your lines. Come Regan, come Cordelia, we need to be together on this." She tugged both sisters by the sleeve and drew them aside from the rest of the group.

"As we all know, our father is resolved to divide his kingdom into three today. But what we don't know yet is which of us gets which region."

"Well, we know we don't know that already..." Regan started to interrupt, but Goneril cut across her.

"Just shut up. We haven't got much time. There are only a couple of caveats to us each getting a good share. The silly old fool wants us to declare our love for him before he divvies up. And afterwards he says he will take it in turns to live with us, a third of the year each."

"What sort of declaration?" Regan looked puzzled.

"Oh," Goneril replied, a little irritation showing in her voice. "That's the easy bit. Something like 'Sir, I love you more than words can wield the matter... blah, blah blah... a love that makes breath poor, and speech unable, beyond all manner of so much I love you.'

There, something along those lines—only you make your own words up."

"I was never very good at speeches," Regan replied. "I hope you go first; then I can just follow you. Or I could say something like..." she drew a deep breath, before saying with dramatic hand wringing, and a heaving bosom.

"'I am alone felicitate in your dear Highness's love.' There Cordy, beat that."

Cordelia looked at both of them in horror.

"How can you say things like that? Of course we love him—he is our father and our king—but what about any love for our husbands, and future children? Aren't we supposed to love and enjoy their company too, maybe even more?"

"Now don't play the drama queen with us, Cordy." The words were jocular, but the tone was threatening, as Goneril looked down on her younger sister. "It's thinking like that that could cost us our rights."

"Our father won't be swayed by empty protestations," Cordelia replied, confidently. "Of course we love him according to our bond to him as a father and a king. What more is there? What more can there be? Your fancy words won't stop him from doing what he knows is right. You'll see."

Goneril was about to respond, but her voice was drowned by a fanfare of trumpets and a servant arrived bearing the king's crown on a cushion Then the king himself entered with his retinue, one of whom was carrying a large map of the kingdom. Cordelia caught her breath as she noticed the Duke of Burgundy and the King of France on either side of her father.

Everyone bowed or curtseyed as the king paused, regally, to acknowledge the presence of his daughters and their husbands. Cordelia noted, with admiration, how, despite his age, he still looked every inch a king; how his presence could still dominate those around him. It's going to be all right, she thought, he's still got it. She allowed herself to relax a little.

Lear smiled as he turned to one of his entourage.

"The stage is set?" he asked. The gentleman in waiting bowed low again.

"It is indeed my liege. The Earls, Gloucester and Kent, are already there."

The old king nodded, pleased with what he heard.

"Then let us proceed."

Without further word he drew himself up to his full majestic height, swirling his cloak around him. His attendants pulled back the curtain as, followed by his three daughters, the Dukes of Albany, Cornwall and Burgundy, the King of France, and the rest of his retainers, he swept into the great hall.

Look to the Lady

Inverness

My Darling,

Oh, how I have missed you from my bed these last few nights. Now I have risen and the day is half gone, yet I still burn with desire to have you by my side. And have you satisfy my thirst for news.

I don't know whether it is worth writing to you, as the battle may well be over by now, and you will be here-before I finish, but I must do something to pass the time, or I will go mad.

War keeps you from me, and my body yearns for you. I am, at the same time, filled with such dread for your safety, my noble lord, and with eager anticipation of your good fortune. Maybe, even as I write, this war will have taken you from me. But, I cannot suppress a confidence that all has gone well for you on the field and we will go on to greater things which will bring us ever closer than before. Will this war be the gateway to our prosperous future? Or the end of the House of Glamis? Only God, or the fates, can tell us—if we have wit to understand their meaning. So I have prayed to God nightly for your safe deliverance, and our future together.

How has the battle gone? And has the treacherous Cawdor been caught and executed? How one can be so deceived in people! He struck me as a fine and noble lord; a gentleman of open honesty. But how the king, my brother-in-law was duped by him! I hope that you, my noble lord, have acquitted yourself with valour on the field of battle so that my dear brother, Duncan, will recognise you with something more substantial than glowing words. What use are these if they are not accompanied by power and titles? For you and I, my lord, are not destined to end our days in this draughty castle, mourning our dead babies, and bending the knee to others.

Do I shock you, my sweet lord, with these sentiments? We will talk more when you are safe home, and rested. I know you will not turn the king's praise to our good without me beside you. You are too gentle, too full of the milk of human kindness, to press things home to your own advantage. And yet needs must as befits your deserved destiny, and mine. Such matters cannot be left to chance alone. Sometimes I wish that I could be with you now, at the battle's end, that I could pour my ambitious spirits into your ear. But maybe it is better that I have stayed at home; to greet you here and help you screw your courage to the sticking place so we can, together, claim what should be yours.

Yes, I have had a glass of wine already this morning. But what makes most men drunk, just makes me bold. As a mere woman, a loving wife, I have been bound to stay at home, fretting, and drinking pledges to your good fortune. My love for you is undimmed as I wander restlessly in the night, mourning our lost infants, yearning to bear you more strong, brave men-children as befits your bloodline. Absence only makes the candle burn stronger, and I await your return with impatience, my heart full of desire and expectation, as the light thickens.

Don't deny it. You too are ambitious. WE, both, are ambitious. Ambitious for each other as much as for ourselves. To date, you have practiced service and loyalty to Duncan. You have performed great deeds. Stayed close to him. Been valiant on the field of battle. All this has placed him in your debt so that now, when looking to his natural heir, he should not look towards his wife, my dearest sister, and her family. You, her valiant brother-in-law, are strong and mature, unlike his weakly half grown sons who are not ready for the responsibilities of government. Duncan is old. Why, he looks so like my father in repose, I feel I am his natural heir myself!

I should not harm him, but I do so envy my sister. I feel I was born to be a queen, to be the wife of the king. Why should she have been granted that, and not me? She is a nothing, mousey, person compared to me. He a pallid puppet, made of shadows, compared to you. You my lord, have all the vigour and nobility that befits a king—and I should know! Let us not leave to chance your rightful claim to kingship.

I could write more, but fear I have already revealed too much of my way of thinking. And now I hear knocking at the castle gate. No doubt it is a messenger with letters sent by you, bringing me news, I hope, of your great victory, and promises of your just rewards and elevation. Great tidings such as these, my lord, as befits your noble character, are what I yearn for. With luck, you will be here before nightfall. We are the closest seat to battle and so, God willing, may the king come with you. We will royally entertain him. Though when he goes will be for us to determine!

Word travels fast through the castle and, before I even read you letters, I can thank God that you are safe. I await your coming tonight, my noble lord, with all my love, honour and obedience.

But, for now, I must lay aside my pen, and put this letter safely in my closet. As you are already on your way here, we shall read it together at our leisure. But, for now, I must go and order up a banquet to welcome home my brave lord and master and those royal guests that Fate is bringing to partake of our hospitality.

My blood runs fast with desire to have you beside me again; and my head is full of ideas for our future together.

But I sign off now, your partner in future greatness, and, as ever, your innocent flower and dearest chuck.

Your loving wife
Lady Macbeth

The Ghost Queen

A winter's tale—a tale too far-fetched to be true? A tale befitting a cold winter's night, when friends and families huddle close around roaring fires to tell each other stories of ghosts and magic to while away the long, cold hours before bedtime? Stories of derring-do? Of kings and queens? Of children lost and found? Of the dead returning to visit their families? Of statues coming to life? My story has no heroes or great deeds but, if you have a moment, come close, sit beside me by the hearth, and listen.

I was distraught when Paulina took me back to her house that day, but I thought it would only be for a couple of weeks. Never for a minute did I expect to be there months later, let alone years. Sixteen in fact. Sixteen long years of pretending to be dead.

He'd abused me, Paulina said. Dear, wise Paulina; my rock and guide when I had no one else to turn to. Your husband must be punished for what he has done to you, she would say. And I must take time to recover, and decide what I wanted to do with the rest of my life.

I still loved him then, of course, and couldn't see what had happened to me was abuse. Surely, that is when someone punches and kicks you? Yet, he had never laid a finger on me. Not once. No, he always behaved towards me with manners befitting a king. Though sometimes...often... if I disappointed or upset him, he would be angry. But, I would tell myself, I should have been more careful, more attentive to his needs, more submissive. After all, a head of state has many pressures and calls upon his time. His home—his palace—should be a haven from such stresses. And, somehow, I kept on failing him.

As I became older and wiser, and better read, I could see what Paulina meant. I was never going to be the wife and queen he thought he wanted. Looking back, I can see now that, at times, his temper was so violent I was lucky, when he punched the walls and cushions near me, that he never hit me by accident. At the time, all I worried about was that I must have done something really big to upset him; that it was my fault. But as the years rolled on, and Paulina and I chatted through many a long night, I came to understand what she meant by 'abuse.' In truth, as she said, he was always in control of his temper, and his intention was to frighten and subdue me. But it was wrong, even for a king, to expect his wife to live in constant fear.

He is penitent now of course, and believes he has lost everything he once held dear. But I have never felt I could just emerge from the shadows as if nothing was wrong before he 'killed' me, however remorseful he appeared to be. Paulina was right and he really did deserve to suffer for what he brought upon himself and all his family, not least his wife. Though sixteen years pretending you don't exist, had been a bit hard on me too.

Most of the first few months with Paulina, especially right at the beginning, when I was so ill she thought I really would die, I wished my life would end. Where did a woman go, what was there to live for, if your husband hated you as much as Laertes seemed to hate me? If he accused you of carrying his best friend's baby, had the baby taken away from you and ordered it to be killed? If he stopped you seeing your darling son? And if you then heard that the poor little boy had died of grief because he missed you, his mother, so much? My good name, my home, my children, and everyone else that I loved, which still included my husband then, was gone forever.

So, for months, I went to bed each night in the tiny

secluded cottage on Paulina's estate and prayed to God that I wouldn't wake up. But I did, and wept with despair each morning to find myself still alive. And it was so much worse if the sun was shining and the birds were singing. What right had they to be so cheerful when I was so unhappy?

Sixteen whole years in limbo. *Why? What had I done wrong?* I had married young, and grown to love my husband, whatever that meant. You didn't marry for love when dynasties and kingdoms were at stake; that was a decision your father made for you, as my father did for me. But he chose well, I thought. And everybody said it was a good match. Laertes was a prince and heir to the throne of Sicilia, and I was a princess with a substantial dowry. Laertes was handsome and clever, and I was said to be a beauty; not for nothing was I named after Hermione, the daughter of the legendary Helen of Troy. I had been well tutored too, by my mother, in the ways of being a queen and, even though I was young, I was confident I could be an ideal wife and model consort for a monarch.

Ah, the naivety of the young!

Laertes was clever, as I said, quick witted, and fun to be around when he was in the mood. And he would want me to join in, help him entertain his friends, play the perfect hostess—that kind of thing. Anything that helped maintain the party atmosphere. But one thing I quickly learnt was to monitor his moods, for when he was out of sorts he would take it out on those close to him: friends, servants, and—of course—me.

One step wrong and he would freeze me out. Sometimes a mood would last for months. But when I tried to find out from him what I had done wrong, and how I could make amends, he would go pale with anger, and smash my ornaments, or tear my dresses. He told me I was ugly so often that I came to believe him rather than believe my friends and ladies in waiting, like dear Paulina, who would try to restore my confidence by reminding me that I was still regarded as the most beautiful woman in the kingdom.

I lived in dread of his disapproval, and did my best always to please him, but always I had to choose my words carefully, or bite my tongue, to avoid upsetting him. I schooled myself to believe this was the right thing to do. In the end he was the king, I told myself, and kings were used to being obeyed, without people crossing them. That was just how it was, he was my lord and master, and my king. And I loved him. Back then, I really and truly did.

So, I would do anything to keep him in good humour and lived for his rare words of praise. I know he was pleased when he became a father, and very happy that our first born was a beautiful, little boy. I did my best to have more children for him, but it took some years of trying. Initial success followed by bitter disappointments as again and again, after just a few months, each pregnancy came to nothing. I was ashamed of myself and I really did understand why he felt angry and bitter as one miscarriage followed another. I was excited when, at last, I found I was actually going to carry a baby to term. I thought he was too.

It wasn't out of character for him to invite his oldest friend, Polixenes, the King of Bohemia, to stay. After all, he enjoyed entertaining and he hadn't spent much time with this friend since they were boys. They had maintained a regular correspondence however and, as both kingdoms were enjoying a rare period of simultaneous peace and prosperity, they could afford to take some time together. But then I fell pregnant, and knowing how precarious my previous pregnancies had been, and how keen he was to have a second heir, I was surprised that he chose to press his friend to stay on, and wanted me to attend all the feasts and help to entertain him.

Polixenes seemed only too happy to stay on. And on. Nine whole months it was before he was, finally, adamant that he had to return to his own country. Even then, Laertes tried to get him to stay longer. When he failed, he ordered me to try to persuade him. I was really tired. The baby was due shortly, my head ached, my feet were swollen, I had indigestion, I didn't feel I could face another banquet, and I hardly had enough energy to entertain my little son, let alone a couple of kings, so I could have done without having guests around any longer. But Polixenes was a lovely man, and he was my husband's greatest friend, so I put aside my own yearning for peace and rest, and summoned up my most charming wiles to coax him to stay on.

It wasn't that hard, to be honest, a few gentle words of encouragement and a smile, and Polixenes agreed to stay another week. I glowed with the anticipatory pleasure of delivering to my husband something that he was certain to be glad about. Yes, I really thought Laertes would be pleased with me for succeeding where he had not. But that was not to be.

Instead, his mood turned in an instant, and he became angry and upset with both me and his dear friend. I really could not understand what I was supposed to have done wrong, after all I had succeeded in what he had asked me to do. Maybe, by now, I should have known better than expect him to praise or thank me for it, but even I was dismayed to find that he perceived my 'success' as proof of disloyalty to him. Nay, that he was an innocent victim, a dupe even, to my prolonged misconduct. For him, the fact that Polixenes only agreed to stay because I asked him was evidence of adultery between Polixenes and me; that we had in fact shown him up to be a cuckold. The shock of his accusations was like a blow in the stomach. I felt humiliated. No, more than that, mortified.

Before nightfall, and despite anything that I or his courtiers could say, my husband had convinced himself that his friend and I had actually been having an affair from the moment Polixenes arrived in the country. Worse, that the baby I was carrying, was Polixenes's not his. Laertes should have known that this was not possible and I tried to reason with him, but that just seemed to make him worse. Others tried to reason with him, but he became even more driven by his own convictions and declared his intent to have his old friend killed. This was too much even for Laertes's loyal courtiers, and one of his previously most devoted servants hurried to give a warning to Polixenes that the king now wished him dead. I was relieved to hear that he had got away safely but, to Laertes, when he heard about it, it was just further proof of his friend's adultery with me, and of my malign influence over his courtiers.

Banished from his sight, and thrown into prison, I was grateful for the loyalty of my own ladies in waiting and, some weeks early, I gave birth to my beautiful little girl. I was still anxious to please the king in any way I could, and I peered into her sweet little face to find conclusive signs of Laertes's looks. I knew it was his baby, knew that he should realise this too, but if only I could detect in her his eye or hair colouring, his nose shape, his way of smiling. Anything to convince him of my fidelity to him.

Alas, as all my ladies said, the baby was a miniature copy of me in every detail, not her father. And that, at the moment, wasn't going to help the situation although, Paulina, when she took the poor poppet to her father, did her best to make him see similarities between himself and his daughter. In fact, I'm told, she said the baby was the worse for looking just like him. But he still insisted the baby was not his and ordered that she be taken from Paulina, and thrown on the fire.

Burned!

Paulina had by this time been ejected from the court, but her husband remained there and tried to persuade him otherwise. Eventually, Laertes relented a little and agreed to allow him to take the baby out of the country, and abandon her in some far-away place, where she could take her chance on surviving.

And that's the last I heard about my poor baby daughter, and the last Paulina heard about her husband. He set sail with the baby straight away, and no one has heard from him or any of the sailors since. Not for over sixteen years.

It seemed that Laertes was utterly convinced of my guilt, but wanted concrete evidence. He therefore sent ambassadors to the oracle at Delphi for confirmation. Meanwhile, I languished in prison. Some weeks later, his ambassadors returned from Delphi, and a test of my guilt was ordered at the palace, during which the oracle's verdict would be read. Such was my despair, and loss of faith in being able to prove my innocence, that I had no expectation that the oracle would redeem me. I was summoned to the palace but I could hardly stand to hear the oracle's pronouncement. I felt so weak since giving birth, and was so fearful of what might be said, that I was trembling uncontrollably as the oracle's first words were read out:

"Hermione is chaste."

There was more, but it was mostly a blur to me, though I remember the prophesy finishing with the words:

"The King shall live without heir if that which is lost is not found."

I had little time to wonder what was meant by this as I fell into a dead faint. Clearly, it was not appropriate to send me back to prison, so I was carried instead to Paulina's home. Here, to protect my sanity, she hid me in this little cottage I'm still living in. You need time, she told me, to recover mentally and physically. And, she added, you need to decide for yourself what you want to do after all these years of being browbeaten. Did I want to retreat to a nunnery, or escape completely from the king and the kingdom? On the other hand, did I, after careful consideration, want to return to my husband? He was, after all, the king, and many people believed that he was truly penitent for the havoc he had caused within his family. *Would that be enough to persuade me to go back?* I needed time to think. Meanwhile, Paulina returned to the court to tell the king that I had died of grief, having never properly recovered from the ordeals he'd put me through.

Paulina was right to buy me time to think. Maybe not sixteen years, it was true, but from the beginning, a life of seclusion suited me so well that it became a habit. As did going from day to day without making any decisions, just living. No, not living exactly, barely existing really, as, very slowly, my mental and physical strength returned, and I gained some inner peace and composure.

Only one thing had stopped me from actually dying from a broken heart, or by my own hand, in those early days. The hope held out by the oracle's last words. My baby daughter was lost, but maybe not dead. *Would she one day be found? Would she one day come looking for me, and if I had disappeared into a nunnery, or another country, would she ever be able to find me? How would she feel if I really was dead? If she returned, would I once more have the motivation to live out in the real world?* All big questions that I pondered as the years slipped by.

Meanwhile, Paulina, who had long ago reconciled herself to the fact that her husband would never return, devoted herself to looking after me. And both of us prayed that the final words of the oracle would, one day, come to pass. I'm sure that Paulina would have liked to believe that her husband would be found, but we both knew that he was not the one to whom the oracle had referred.

***

One evening, almost sixteen years to the day since I "died," I was sewing quietly when Paulina rushed in, a look of wonderment on her face.

"Look out of the window, madam. Look at all the bonfires!"

I stood up quickly and moved to the window. Sure enough the skyline was filled with twinkling braziers. I turned to Paulina who was standing close, staring excitedly at the flames.

"What does it all mean?"

"It means, your majesty, that the prophecy of the oracle is fulfilled. The king's daughter is found. *Your* daughter is found! Oh the news of how is so, is so…, oh, it is hardly credible."

It was rare for Paulina to be lost for words. But what she had said so far had stunned me too. I sat down quickly, feeling light headed.

"My daughter?"

"Oh my lady." Dear, practical, Paulina was so overcome she didn't know what title to give me. "Word is, she was found as a baby by some poor shepherd who brought her up as his own daughter. But, wonder of it! The King of Bohemia's son, of all people, fell in love with her against the king's approval, so they ran away, and now they are all here—Bohemia, his son, your daughter, and… oh it's all too much." She sat down next to me, and dabbed her eyes with a handkerchief. Then she took several deep breaths before continuing,

"And she is just like you, my lady. There can be no doubt about it, even without your old necklace about her neck, and the parchment left with her by my dear husband."

We wept together then. Me with the pure, simple joy of my daughter's discovery. But she, no doubt with thoughts too about her husband. After all, it was he who had taken my baby and, by his actions, saved her life and probably lost his own. I had rarely thought about him for several years, but I knew Paulina hadn't forgotten him for a single day, and her memories must be particularly raw today.

After several minutes, I was able to compose myself and ask her about him.

"And, you, Paulina, was there news for you?"

She knew instantly what I meant.

"Alas, the good shepherd told me he was killed and eaten by a bear moments after he left the baby. And all the ship's crew were drowned in a great storm that same night. My last hopes of seeing him again are gone." She sighed sadly, and her head drooped. Then she jumped up.

"Enough! It is only confirming what I feared all along, and we have cause enough for joy. Your daughter is returned from the dead and now, so must you."

I had grown to like my secluded life. It had never been intended as a permanent solution, and both Paulina and I had felt we would know when the right moment would arrive for it to end. Surely now, if ever, was the perfect time for me to reveal myself as alive and well?

I did so want to see my darling daughter who had been so cruelly snatched from me sixteen years ago. *But what about the others?* I thought of all the people out there I would have to face; all the difficult memories that still haunted me—my husband, Polixenes, courtiers who had grown old and frail in my absence. Then there were the new faces; my daughter and her lover. What had Paulina called them? Perdita and Florizel? Perdita—how apt, for once she had been lost to me. But now she was found. And then there were the once familiar faces who were there no longer. Paulina's husband of course, but mainly my little boy, who would have been a mature man by now had he lived. For me, he would be the biggest absence from the group.

"Paulina, I can't. I simple don't feel strong enough. Not now. Not today. And Laertes, I can't meet him yet. Not now. Maybe tomorrow, when I've grown used to the idea. Or next week…" My voice trailed away.

Paulina said nothing. She just looked at me and the

silence stretched into minutes as I agonised over what to do.

"But my daughter, I can't wait to see her. Oh, Paulina, what's for the best?"

Paulina smiled.

"I have already thought about that. I told everybody at the palace that I had commissioned a statue of you in secret some years ago, lifelike and just as you would be now if you had lived. I told them it is almost ready, though the paint is wet so they mustn't touch it. Rather than go straight to your empty grave to pay their respects, I have promised them that they can come here first to look at your statue."

"But that's nonsense, there is no statue here. It's just me."

"Yes, madam. Just you."

It took me several seconds to understand what she meant. I started to laugh, quietly at first, then loudly, almost hysterically. The idea of being a statue was so ludicrous! Then I started to cry. Paulina meanwhile stood quietly at my side. When my sobbing ceased, she urged me to sit down.

"You've had a shock, your majesty. Sit here quietly whilst it all sinks in. Meanwhile, I will get things ready."

I sat down as I was bidden. I had no idea what she meant by getting things ready, but as I sat, I began to feel that her statue idea was not as bizarre as it first seemed.

I did so want to see my daughter. I was curious, too, to see my husband. *How had he reacted to the sudden arrival of the baby daughter he had once ordered to be burnt? And what of his old friend whom he had also condemned to death? But, when it came to the test, would my dread of my estranged husband, my loathing of what he had done to me in the past, overcome me? Or would the passage of time have calmed my emotions?* He was said to be repentant; to regard me as his one and only wife. Paulina had always assured me that he had never been tempted to re-marry since he lost me. *Would that be enough? Could I bear to speak to him? To let him touch me?* I shrank from the idea. Yet I so wanted to see my precious daughter. And the only way to do that, it seemed, was to go along with Paulina's fantastical plan.

With that, Paulina returned carrying one of my old dresses over her arm. I had not worn it since coming to her house, but I recognised it immediately. It was the dress Laertes had once said suited me well. A rare compliment I had treasured at the time. I knew he would recognise it. Was that what Paulina intended? She saw the question in my eyes and shook her head.

"No indeed, your majesty. I have just seen your daughter, and I fancy she is the spitting image of you when you last wore this. You are still much the same size as you were then. That's why I chose it."

"I'm a lot older and greyer than I was then."

"True," Paulina responded, smiling. "That's why I told them the statue was as you would be now if you had lived. But, your majesty, you are still a beautiful woman. Come along now, we must make haste and get you changed, or they will all be here before we're ready." She took my arm, but then recoiled slightly in surprise. "Why, madam, you are trembling. Here, let me get you some wine to steady your nerves."

Quickly, she poured me a glass of wine. I noticed that she put a large splash of brandy in it too, but I said nothing, just drank it down in one gulp. I shivered and coughed as it coursed through me, but I soon felt calmer and I had stopped shaking by the time Paulina had finished buttoning me into the dress, combing my hair and re-touching my make-up.

She assured me that, as far as all the others were concerned, this new statue of the old Queen Hermione was hers, and hers alone. She alone had commissioned it, and it was to remain with her in her cottage until she died. It was up to me to say if I wanted things to stay that way. From my vantage point as a piece of lifeless stone, I could look on my family and old friends whilst they looked at me. After a short time, she would order them to leave her (us) in peace. Unless, that is, I wanted to return to life. In which case, she would be only too happy to see me go with them.

Once I was ready, Paulina closed the curtains and lit a few candles which cast shadows into all the corners of the room. Then she steered me into the furthermost corner, and threw a light gauze cloth over me, explaining as she did so that, however still I stood, I would still have to breathe, and the veil, together with the flickering shadows from the candles, would conceal any slight movement of my chest. She smiled at me again to re-assure me, and I smiled back. I was going to see my daughter; the baby lost to me over sixteen years ago was now a full grown woman, and I would at long last see her again. Nothing else, for the moment, mattered.

My belief in the oracle's prediction that my daughter would be found had kept me alive, and I must see her, if only the once. She did not know I was alive and, if I chose, I could remain as a lifelike statue in her memory. In the future, I could be like a ghost who could visit her in her dreams; someone she could dream about as and when it pleased her.

Or I could return to the palace with them. All of them; my daughter, my husband, Polixenes, his son and all the courtiers. There could be no half measures. I could not be flesh and blood for one, and a stone replica, a ghost queen, for the others. To think I had had sixteen years waiting and preparing for this moment, yet was still undecided.

Soon there was the sound of footsteps on the path outside and subdued voices. I could clearly recognise my husband's voice, and that of Polixenes, and I could guess at the others.

My mind raced. Even now, I was not sure I had enough self-knowledge and strength to make the right decision, the best decision for me and my daughter. I felt my hands trembling again and willed them to be still.

Paulina noticed and touched my hands briefly. Then she looked at me through the gauze, straight into my eyes. I took a deep breath and the trembling eased.

"Be strong," she urged.

"I will," I assured her.

"It's your choice."

"I know."

There was a knock.

I froze, just like a statue, and Paulina went to the door to let the world in.

Ban, Ban, Cacaliban!

I see my boy, in my mind's eye. Standing on the headland, watching as the ship disappears over the horizon. Gazing after his old master, Prospero, who is heading back to where he belongs, after twelve long years dominating the island rightfully belonging to me, Sycorax the witch, and her descendants. Good riddance to him. The magic he used to outshine mine is spent now, his power over spirits and other humans has been laid to rest, and my freckled whelp is again master of the island in my place. Justice, if you can call it that, at last!

But, what a mooncalf my boy is! How long will he last with no one to tell him what to do; no one to bully him into performing even the simplest chores; no one to chastise him every time, and every day, he fails? For one thing is sure, though I will speak it aloud to no one, that boy needs a firm hand, be it mine, or the damned Prospero's, or he is into mischief of all sorts.

Yee devils! How I have loved to follow my boy's wickedness, and cursed with joy to see him plot to thwart Prospero's plans, especially when he tried to despoil his daughter. What a coup it would have been to see the island peopled by the progeny of my misshapen knave and that sweet-natured, dainty girl. What a way to get back at Prospero, who stole my boy's island from under his scurvy nose.

But Caliban is just too dim, and his attempted rape was quickly thwarted. Prospero simply swatted him away like a deboshed fish. Yes, the boy really is an ignorant monster, scarcely fit to carry logs, never mind father children, or govern an island. But it was his right to rule the island after me and now that everybody else has gone, he can. Now, he's the one in charge.

He'll be lonely; the spirits on the island have dispersed, the humans have sailed away. Just him and any fish, grubs and berries he can forage to keep his gross belly full. I'll not weep for him. What mother could cry over such a thing of darkness? Such a hideous, howling, dim-witted lump of rancid lard, as my son has become?

And yet? And yet I owed my life, such as it was, to him. Back when I lived in Africa, the authorities discovered my witchcraft, a hanging offence. However, they chose to throw me out of Algiers instead of putting me to death because I was pregnant with him. Months before, I had been ravished in lustful fury by a diabolical spirit who then abandoned me to an uncertain fate when he realised he'd impregnated me with his vile sperm. Not for him, the delights and responsibilities of fatherhood. Oh no! But it was this hateful seed in my womb that saved my life when the magistrates accused me of practicing the black arts.

And why shouldn't I? After all, I was Sycorax the witch. I was proud of my black arts, and proud to worship my god, Setebos. What had any Christian ever done for me? Witches were not welcomed in a country where wishy-washy followers of Jesus knelt down before a cradle containing a defenceless baby, and turned the other cheek. Or Mohammedans bent low and prayed to their god, Allah, five times a day. Pah!

Still, it's hard to believe now, that this puppy-headed monster was ever a meek and mewling babe in my arms. From being a tiny hag-seed thrust into my womb, my belly swelled as he grew large within me. But, as the law in Algiers stood then, whilst they could convict me as a witch, they could not hang me as an expectant mother. Instead they exiled me to a distant island where, they had decided in their collective wisdom, I could do as much black magic as I chose, without harming anyone. Except, perhaps, myself or my charmless progeny—and no one cared about either of us.

***

It was a rough voyage for one in my condition, and I cursed the sailors roundly as they dumped me, with nothing but the rags on my back, at the tiny natural harbour to the island, and immediately set sail back to the mainland without a word of farewell. Frightened I would cast a spell on them and put their lives in jeopardy, I suppose. Well, I tried!

In fact, I cast several spells on the beach to create a vicious storm, in the hope they would have a treacherous journey, and their boat would sink. But, although I could control the moon with my curses, and make the tides ebb and flow more erratically, these were not enough to wreck the boat. I called on Setebos to help me, but he was not listening, and would not come to my aid.

Then, alone on that beach, in the rain and wind, as the gritty sand swirled and bit into my feet and hail stones lashed my face, I spawned my only child. I screamed with agony as that ugly, howling monster tore through my womb and burst into the world. A wretched litter of one. I gathered him into my ragged cloak and placed him against my bony chest to suck. I had nothing else I could give him then.

Nothing else, that is, apart from a name, and I decided to call him Caliban. Caliban/Cannibal. I loved him and loathed him simultaneously as only a hag-mother knew how. Each day I fed him bile from my withered dugs, until he was old enough to chew the grubs and berries that thrived around us. From the start, and from the bottom of my witch's heart, I wished him ill in thought and deed. Indeed an evil turn of mind was all I was going to be able to bequeath him. That and the island.

***

When the storm abated, and I had recovered enough from the birth to explore deeper into the island, I found it to be green and pleasant. Not at all a bad place to be exiled to, unless you are a witch who craves bleakness and fog. Aside from rocky outcrops, the soil was fertile, and the climate temperate all year round. There was plenty of wood from the numerous trees with which to make a decent shelter. Also, a choice of fish in the scattered lagoons and surrounding sea, small animals, grubs, nuts and berries all year round. At least I knew we would never starve.

But it was a dull life for one used to dishing out a daily dose of devilment. I missed the company of other witches, the twilight meetings round a steaming cauldron, the sharing of spells and successful sorcery. The temperate climate quickly started to bore me. I tired too, of my son's constant demands. He was an ignorant monster right from a baby and, as he got older, he became rougher and more violent. He would have been truly frightening to anyone meeting him for the first time, had he not been so stupid. Yet, it seemed, no matter what I did to him, however much I neglected him, he never raised his voice or fists against me directly. He loved me, poor sod. I suppose I must have loved him too, in my own way, or surely I would have strangled him at birth.

There were few natural storms on the island. Sometimes, when I was bored, or fed up beyond endurance with my own company, or Caliban was driving me to my wits' end with his shrieking and clumsy ways, I would conjure up a storm, go out onto the headland and watch for ships that might be wrecked upon the rocky shore. I yearned to see some poor sailors tossed about in the angry surf, crying out for help before sinking under the waves. At least this would have been a diversion from the monotony of life on the island. It would have provided me with some sport, and company of a sort. But alas, no ships ever came close enough to the island to fall under one of my spells.

What did happen from time to time were occasional bursts of music. They seemed to come from out of thin air, and were certainly none of my doing. Melodious harmonies, like a thousand twanging instruments, humming around my ears, and sweet airs to penetrate even a witch's stone heart. No, I could never conjure up such things of beauty, and had never wanted to. But at times they were the only thing that would calm my son when he was in one of his violent rages. Music that would make him fall into a deep sleep. Then he'd wake up and cry to be asleep again. It seemed he preferred sleeping and dreaming to this music, to being a grateful son for his mother, and learning from her wickedness.

Caliban and I were the only corporate beings on the island. But we were not completely alone, as the air was full of spirits. Maybe they created the music, but I doubt it—they were a pretty feeble lot, all ethereal, and insubstantial wafting, unable to learn witchcraft, and only partially susceptible to it. They didn't trouble me much, but it made me spit that I couldn't control them, and get them to serve me.

I tried with one who seemed a quick witted sprite. He called himself Ariel, and I cast enough of a spell on him to get him to work for me. But, for all his airy agility, he was truculent, and had no aptitude for evil. Worse than useless in fact as, by the time I realised he was not going to be of any use to me, I had already taught him some of my spells, and I was afraid of what he would do with such knowledge.

What to do? I couldn't just release him back to the world of the spirits, as who knew what harm he and his fellow sprites could do to me and my son if they put their minds to it. I decided to kill him, and called on Setebos to help me. But I found to my dismay that my spells were no longer strong enough for this. They could hurt him, and make him cry out, but the next day he would be up and airborne, like a seed from a dandelion. I could imprison him though, and one day, whilst he was still weak from one of my spells, I gathered him up and thrust him into the trunk of a pine tree. I told him he would stay there till he agreed to obey me fully. Then, and only then would I consider releasing him. But he was stubborn, refused to agree and, as my memory started to play tricks on me, I forgot the spells I would need to release him.

Despite the balmy climate, the plentiful food and wholesome water readily available on the island, I became frail and sick. Or maybe because of it. It wasn't the kind of setting in which a witch can thrive normally, and trying to create my own weekly tonic of miasma was becoming too exhausting. I was getting old, and Caliban was almost an adult, or as grown-up as he was ever going to be. Imprisoning Ariel had taken more of my powers than I had expected, and left me listless. I found I missed even the few tasks he did for me.

Maybe I should have got Caliban to do more. Although still clumsy and dull-witted he had become big and strong. As I grew weaker, I tried to get him to fetch the food, and even cook it. He never learnt to cook anything edible, but he was happy enough to go off and search for food. However, as time went by, his hunting forays seemed to go on for longer and longer. The power balance between us was changing. Once he realised I couldn't go after him with a whip, and my ability to cast spells to cause him pain was waning, I had very little hold over him. He was too stupid to see for himself what he needed to do to keep me alive, and how important I still was to him.

"Be back by nightfall!" I instructed him one day as he set off on another hunting foray. He grunted and gave me one of his oafish grins as he headed towards the lake on the other side of the island where I know he loved to lark about and catch the occasional fish. I knew then, as I saw him skipping, and tripping, over fallen logs, and bellowing with joy, that I would be lucky to see him before dawn the next day, if then. I was starving, my heart was failing, my mind was turning to mush and, by the time he returned two days later with nothing but a putrefying fish under his arm, I was dead.

He was sorry then. They were genuine tears I think, as he looked down on my shrunken, crumpled body. But he wasn't sad for long. The poor oaf didn't understand that I had starved to death whilst he was away enjoying himself. Still, he had enough wit to dig a hole and bury me, along with the now stinking fish. Then he cried a bit more, wiped his nose on his filthy sleeve and went fishing again. He never gave a moment's thought to the spirit Ariel locked up in the tree trunk. But then, he was powerless to unlock him even if he'd wanted to. The ignorant monster had been too stupid to learn any of my spells.

So I died with an evil deed still in place, and found myself in purgatory along with all the other unrepentant witches whose lives had ended with their sins outstanding. Ariel too, was locked in a sort of purgatory. Not of his own making, of course, and I can't say I grieved much over this.

I can't work out how many years he remained locked in that tree, weeping and wailing to the empty air, struggling to be free, but without the physical strength to crack open the tree trunk, or the magic spells to conjure back his liberty.

He would have remained in there forever if that wretched human hadn't arrived out of the blue, with a trunk of books, a smart cloak, and a small daughter. Yes, If that damned Prospero hadn't been exiled to the island as an outcast from his own lands by people who, like my tormentors in Algiers, wanted to get rid of him, but hadn't the stomach to kill him, Ariel would have continued to live in a limbo just as wretched as my after-life has been.

I laughed when I first saw him. The man seemed so pathetic with nothing to assist him, not even a spade, or other tools, to build a shelter. Just a pile of old books. My hovel was in a pretty awful state with only Caliban to tend to it by this time. For anyone other than my son, it was uninhabitable. So this man, with his tiny daughter in tow, was going to have to set to quickly if he was going to be able to feed and clothe and house the both of them, and I couldn't see how he was going to do that.

Prospero's life on the island started like a mirror of mine with my son those many years ago. Here was a 'good' man with a 'sweet' daughter, in contrast to my evil witchery and oafish offspring. But I doubted if they could manage better than Caliban and I had. Despite its charms, the island was no place for dreamers. I sensed, with glee, that they were doomed. Prospero, he called himself, but I couldn't see how he was going to live up to his name and prosper on the island. What use is goodness and virtue without other resources?

Curses! I was mistaken. Those books he'd brought with him were full of magic. Good, strong, magic. With them he could control the elements and he soon had a shelter built. Within days he had discovered the imprisoned sprite. He quickly looked up the right spell to set him free. Well free after a fashion—Ariel had to work for him then, as he had been supposed to work for me. This time round though the spirit worked more or less willingly.

Prospero came across my abominable monster of a son in the first week and I could see, at once, who would be the master and who the servant. But Prospero was a gentle master and was happy let my son be. He treated him kindly, and fed him and even tried to teach him his letters in return for work around their settlement. I could see that Caliban was transferring his love for me to him, and was in danger of settling down contentedly to a life of serfdom unless I did something to stop it. I still had some power to do evil beyond the grave, and I decided I must use it.

Again, I called on Setebos to help me and, together, we put lustful thoughts into Caliban's head. Dirty ideas about sex and Prospero's daughter. What a coup it would be if we could thwart Prospero's taming of Caliban and, at the same time, rob his darling daughter of her virtue. Do it son, when Prospero is not looking, we urged across the ether. Grab her, take her, deflower her, and plant the seeds of your own progeny in her womb. Make her your servant and wife. Strike your blow against the usurping Prospero. If you succeed, he will have to live on despising is own grandchildren. Or kill them.

Setebos and I willed it, and we nearly succeeded. But, alas, Miranda screamed out. Prospero rushed in and Caliban was caught with his trousers down, so to speak. Prospero's rage was such that I thought he would kill my boy on the spot. But no. Instead he was made to work even harder, ordered to sleep outside the hut, forbidden to go near Miranda, and plagued with agonising aches and pains if ever he argued or did things wrong. Poor boy, as he was always doing things wrong, his life became one of constant torment.

Prospero stole the island from my son and thwarted my son's lust for his pretty daughter. Both things were bad enough, but he had still more ways of reaching out to torment me in my after-life. His spells were always more effective than mine. Like when he found the spirit Ariel bound inside the tree, he released him so easily. I'm sure I could have done that too, if I'd managed to remember the right spell. I just hadn't got round to it before I died. Perhaps the spirit would have been properly grateful to me then, and I could have forced him to obey me, for fear I would return him to captivity if he crossed me again. But Prospero released him, so the wretch was grateful to him instead. It hardly needed any threats or spells from Prospero to get him to serve willingly.

Still, I couldn't help noticing that, as the years went by, Ariel started to grow restless. Prospero kept him working more or less willingly, by promising him his freedom one day. Just not yet. And the poor sap believed him, and even helped him with his magic. I could see tensions growing, nonetheless. Who would break first? There was no doubt in my mind that Prospero would win any confrontation, but I relished the prospect of a battle of wills between them. Anything to relieve the constant tedium of my life in limbo.

Years went by and maybe Prospero was also growing bored on the island. Or maybe he was just looking ahead, to the time when his daughter would be fully grown up, and needing a husband. He would have to look further than the island for one of those, as he would never have considered my boy, even without the attempted rape.

***

I could sense dramatic changes were afoot even before he used his spells, one day, to cause a major shipwreck. This brought his brother, and others who had conspired in his usurpation and exile to the island. His magic, always so much stronger than mine, managed to wreck their ship without doing any damage; drown the occupants yet let all live; find and test a suitable suitor for his daughter; bring his erstwhile enemies to a state of remorse; and finally arrange to sail back with them to regain his old dukedom. That last bit was news to me. In all his ruminations on the island, he had never talked about what he had lost. I thought he was just a human wizard, not a nobleman.

It was an eventful day, that day he caused that shipwreck. Hard to believe so much could happen in such a short space of time. But it did, and by evening he was ready to set sail across a flat azure coloured sea, under a cloudless sky, along with his daughter, her new fiancé, and all the other humans.

He found time before going to bid farewell to the spirits, and the blasted Ariel was finally granted all the freedom he could possibly want. Prospero's last act, before clambering onto the boat, was to cast his books of magic and precious wand into the sea. What a waste! But they'd have been no use to my feeble minded son and I knew I could never get back from Limbo to use them.

So my son is now alone on the island. That small, strange, enchanted isle. Magic abounds all round him but out of the reach of my ignorant monster. I watch him as he stares out at the departing ship, and I think I see a tear run down his cheek as his shoulders sag. His mother's witchcraft is spent, his human master has broken his wand and sailed away. *How will he cope, now he has no one to keep him in order? How will he pass what's left of his little life?* He is free now, with no one to boss him about, or to inflict pain on him. At last he is the master of all he surveys. Master of nothing.

About Margaret Egrot

Margaret Egrot is the author of two novels for young adults, as well as several short stories and plays for adults. After sitting through countless Shakespeare plays as a child, and studying him at school and university, she admired, rather than loved his work. Then, in 2012, she was runner-up in the Royal Shakespeare Company – Cross Pens inaugural play writing competition, and her prize included the Complete Works of William Shakespeare, a notebook, and a pen. Subsequently she decided to re-read all his plays, and is still happily working her way through his canon.

Social Media links

Amazon author pages:
http://www.amazon.co.uk/-/e/B00RVO1BHO
http://www.amazon.com/-/e/B00RVO1BHO

Facebook:

https://www.facebook.com/Margaret-Egrot-1374506486178952/

Twitter: https://twitter.com/meegrot

Blog: www.writingandbreathing.wordpress.com

Acknowledgements

Special thanks, as always, to the Solstice team for their guidance and encouragement.

If you enjoyed this story, check out these other Solstice Publishing books by Margaret Egrot:

And Alex Still Has Acne

Life for fourteen year old Alex is OK most of the time. He enjoys school, has a best friend Sam, and a pretty and only mildly irritating younger sister, Nicky. But then Sam starts acting strangely, and so does Nicky – and both insist on sharing secrets with him and making him promise not to tell anyone. Then Nicky goes missing and only Alex feels he knows where to find her. But is Sam anywhere around to help?

http://www.bookgoodies.com/a/B00RU1Y0G

Girl Friends

Nothing is working out for Courtney, and even Grace, her beautiful best friend, has no time for her now she has a boyfriend who has promised to get her a modelling contract. Courtney senses something is wrong – what is Grace getting herself into? And can Courtney and some new-found friends rescue Grace before it is too late?

http://bookgoodies.com/a/B01EX9DPMS

Love in Waiting

Why is Caro dressing so carefully? Why does she have a copy of James Joyce's Ulysses in her bag? And who is this man in a coma on midsummer's day?

http://bookgoodies.com/a/B00ZPJZNJO

Sleeping Beauty

A teenager told fairy tales by her dying mother, runs away
from her wicked stepmother and into the front of a car.
What will it take to get her out of her year-long coma?

http://bookgoodies.com/a/B01CKKNG7Q